LOVE COMES FULL CIRCLE

KIM A MARCH

For my husband, Paul.

1

CONTRACT

What did he just say? Madeline Sorrells stared at her father in utter disbelief.

"Madeline." He started again, his hand massaging between his eyes. "I know how you must hate me. But...my debts are many. I have no other choice. Shelton is demanding payment—I don't have it." Sighing heavily, he let his hand fall to his lap and looked away from his daughter.

"Father, how could you?" Madeline's face turned red as the heat rose into her cheeks. "I am not a piece of property that you can *somehow* lose in a bet! I am your *daughter*!"

"Shelton demands payment!" He repeated. "You are it. If you don't marry him, he will have me killed. Don't you *understand?*" Her father inhaled deeply. The gray circles under his eyes spoke of little sleep. "It's settled. The man has arrived and will fetch you...tomorrow...morning." He bowed his head and rose. "I am sorry." He whispered as he turned away and walked out, leaving Madeline gaping after him

Joseph Sorrells was a weak and hollow man. But he wasn't always that way. At one time, he had been a loving and doting father who provided very well for his family. He owned the local mercantile and was an upstanding citizen. He was full of life and a God-fearing man. Now, he was just a shell of the man he used to be. His whole world had revolved around a person, his wife. And without her, nothing else mattered. His store, his daughter, his faith...all discarded.

Madeline saw that eight years ago. Her mother died giving birth to a long-awaited son, a son who was also lost. Eliza Sorrells was the anchor of the family. Her faith and trust in God rang true even to her dying breath.

"He is sovereign Joseph...trust in Him." Madeline heard her mother whisper to her father as she slipped away. But instead of trusting God, he hid his sorrows in a bottle. His world shattered. His wife, whom he cherished and adored, was lost to him. The promise of a son, stolen. He didn't want to feel the pain...the loss. So, he kept himself numb with alcohol. All this Madeline understood now, but, at the time, she only felt the hurt and rejection. He shut her out of his life. He couldn't bear to look at the one that shared the image of his beloved Eliza. Madeline needed him to acknowledge and console her, but he was too lost within himself to see her grief. So, at the tender age of ten, she lost her mother, brother, *and* her father.

Joseph had to have heard her crying in the night, calling out for her mother, but he would turn a deaf ear and drink all the more. Some of the ladies from the church tried to fill the gap in Madeline's life. They made sure she attended school and church regularly. They saw to it that she had a young ladies' upbringing to the best of their ability. They begged Joseph to embrace his daughter, the only family he had left, but his sorrow and bitterness ran too deep.

Over the months that followed, he lost the mercantile and further shut himself off from the community. He needed money for liquor and to put food on the table. So, he turned to gambling. He started selling anything of value. He was hooked. He would ride to the next town, and the next, trying to "win the jackpot." Usually, he just came up empty-handed, but even when he did win, it would just end up back on the gambling table. He began racking up debts all over the county. Eventually, some men came collecting. The first time, they took what was left of the silver. Next time they took what remained of his wife's jewels. Then it was the horses, including Madeline's beloved mare, Skye—the list went on, which brought them to this point. They had nothing left, and now it appeared as though he had gambled away his daughter.

MADELINE RAN out into the gloomy night crying, more from anger than anything else. She ran hard, and she ran far, stopping only after her lungs felt like they might burst. She collapsed to the damp ground. Thoughts of hate toward her father for not loving her and anger at God for taking her mother away when she needed her so desperately plagued her mind. She felt like that ten-year-old girl again...lost, scared, and alone. Her sweet, beautiful mother would know just what to say to soothe Madeline's fears. She was always there to make the monsters go away with her calm, gentle voice singing songs of Jesus. Mother's kisses healed many a skinned knee and elbow. But she wasn't here now to make everything better...and Madeline felt like she was reliving her death all over again. Eliza Sorrells would never have let this happen. Of course, if she were still living, her father would never have gambled or drank, and they wouldn't be in this predicament. At that thought, her mind slammed back to her father.

Why should she have to pay for his vices? She looked up and raised her fists to heaven. "It's not fair God! Do you hear me?"

She knew the love of her father for ten wonderful years, but the last eight years had all but erased those cherished memories. He was not that man any longer. They had both suffered the same loss. Couldn't he see that? Instead of comforting her and letting himself be comforted, he turned into a weak, drunken, gambling fool. And she hated him for it. He would bow to this Mr. Shelton, and *she* would pay the price.

She thought of leaving in the night. Never to return— but where would she go? She felt like a caged animal. Her eyes darted all around—her mind and heart racing. She wanted to run further into the cloudy gray night and escape. But then her thoughts began to slow. What would happen to her father if she did? "Oh, I don't care!" Even as she said it, she knew she did. He was all she had left in the world.

Forcing herself to stand, she tried to walk. But she just couldn't. She felt so heavy, burdened down. "God, Your Word says," 'Your yoke is easy. Your burden is light.' It's not feeling very light at the moment."

The tears started to flow again. "What am I going to do? To marry a man I don't know...a gambling man... a man that would have my father killed if I don't go through with it. Oh, father! What have you done?" She covered her face in her hands, sobbing, and sank to the ground again. Bitter tears flowed. She was trapped, and she knew it. She kicked and pounded her fists into the ground like a four-year-old child demanding her way. It didn't appear that God was amused, because, at that moment, it started to rain, soaking the rest of her already damp dress. She sat up suddenly and let the rain mingle with her tears. Her sobs dissipated, and her thoughts cleared. "I'm not alone, am I God? You are always with me..."

"...Where can I go from Thy Spirit? Or where can I flee from Thy presence?
If I ascend to heaven, Thou are there; if I make my bed in Sheol, behold, Thou art there.
If I take the wings of the dawn, if I dwell in the remotest part of the sea,
Even there, Thy hand will lead me, and Thy right hand will lay hold of me."
Psalm 139:7-11

That was a Scripture Madeline's mother taught her when she was five years old and terrified of the dark. Her mother's sweet voice, always comforting, would tell her, "Madeline, God is your closest and dearest friend. Think of Him often, and pray to Him continually. No matter what this life holds, He cares for you and loves you very much!"

"But not as much as Mama, right Mama?" Madeline would ask.

"Oh yes, precious one, even more than Mama. And that's a lot, isn't it?" Her mother would hug her tightly and plant soft kisses all over her face.

Finally resigned...Madeline gathered up her sopping dress and began her dreaded trek back home.

It's in God's hands now. There is nothing to be done about it. I will leave this place and everything I've known behind tomorrow. She sniveled. "God, I still won't be happy about it, and I can't promise there won't be any more fits, but I will try to trust in You. I have to say; my future looks awfully bleak. I pray Mr.

Shelton will be a fine husband. This is not how I always pictured my life going. I wanted to fall deeply in love with the man I was to marry." And as an afterthought said, "...Or at least see him first!"

Though chilled from the rain, she felt cleansed and loved by God. She didn't understand Him at all, why He would allow such a thing, but she knew He loved her.

Another favorite Scripture of her mother's popped into her head.

"Trust in the Lord with all your heart and lean not on your own understanding,
but in all your ways acknowledge Him, and He will direct your paths."
Proverbs 3:5-6

"All right, all right. I hear You!" Madeline squared her shoulders and headed back into the house.

2

SOLITUDE

David was anxious to get this trip over. His debt would be paid at the end of it. He was the younger brother of Richard Shelton, but not many would call them family. The two brothers were different as night and day.

Richard, 30 years old, was a harsh, relentless businessman. He became very rich and powerful—rich in money, property, and valuables but severely lacking in morals. He owned several gambling parlors and saloons in Colorado, Utah, and Nevada. Initially, he had gone into business with some other gentlemen, but Richard didn't like sharing the profits, so over some time, he systematically gave each one the option of getting out, or becoming buzzard food.

David found out the hard way just how harsh his brother could be. At the age of 21, he made some serious mistakes. He got caught up in gambling and accumulated such a massive debt; he ended up signing over his part of Belle Rive (the family ranch) to his brother. In addition, he had to work for Richard as one of his 'collectors.' Whenever

some poor, old sap owed money to Richard, David was sent
to collect. If the money wasn't available, he took other things
of value. One way or another, the debt was paid. Richard
had others working for him too, but David was his favorite
collector—probably because he knew how it grated against
his God-fearing nature.

Most of the work didn't sit right with David. He was
trying to keep his life straight, to live for God—had been for
nearly three years now. He did everything we was told
unless it went against God's Word. Richard often teased
him, saying, "You'll never make a good businessman, little
brother. Gotta have that cut-throat mentality. Not that
yellow-bellied religious balderdash!" He had no tolerance
for the things of God. David made the mistake of 'preaching'
at him once and nearly lost an eye as Richard slung a
whiskey bottle at him.

Now, at 25, the end was in sight for David. He could
hardly keep himself on track. "Freedom!" he shouted to the
desolate hills. It was so close he could taste it. When this trip
was over, he would get far away from his brother and his
past—maybe Dakota territory. Belle Rive was where he had
grown up, but it no longer resembled the beloved place of
his childhood. His parents had died of consumption when
he was 12, which left his 17-year-old lecherous brother in
charge. Since then, Belle Rive had become a place of greed,
drunkenness, and lust.

Over the years, David had been sent to collect money,
horses, jewelry—you name it. But never before had he been
sent to "collect" a person—more specifically, a woman—a
wife for Richard. He scoffed at the thought. Apparently, the
girl's father had run up such a massive gambling debt, and
couldn't pay it off, that Richard agreed to take the daughter

as his wife for payment. Poor girl...to have such a father, and then to marry such a man! *Oh well! Last job, and I'm free! That's all that matters now.* So he kept telling himself. Though, if he were truthful, none of this sat well with him.

He was headed to Colorado this time. The journey from Colorado to his home in Nevada would typically take a little less than a month, but with a female in tow...it could be never-ending. With that thought, he decided he had better enjoy the solitude and quiet before she joined him. *Boy, will that be a lonnnngggg ride home.*

IN ALL HIS JOURNEYS, David had become a pretty good tracker and hunter. He could traverse pretty stealthily through all kinds of terrain and eat very well along the way. One fortunate encounter with a Cheyenne named "Soars with Eagles," taught him much about how to survive in all kinds of adversity, which is what the Cheyenne had to do to exist. The US Cavalry was trying to conquer these proud people and put them on what's called a reservation. (Where they wouldn't be a "nuisance" any longer.) The reservation represented death to their way of life—their traditions, their freedom.

Freedom is what David craved more than anything. He couldn't imagine being forced to live like that. He had, on more than one occasion, helped his friend, Soars with Eagles, and others, by leading the Cavalry off their trail.

From time to time as he traveled, he stayed with these generous people. They gave him the name Hat' êstseahe, which means "bushy head," because of his curly hair.

Soars with Eagles took him on a buffalo hunt with them once. David watched as some of the men and women drove the buffalo toward several men waiting with their bows and arrows. He learned how they use most of the buffalo parts for tools, toys, blankets, storage vessels, and other things so that virtually nothing went to waste.

On another visit, Soars with Eagles found David sitting among the women watching them with fascination, as they embroidered knife sheaths from porcupine quills. He teased and jeered him for three days. At the end of the week, David received one of the splendid knife sheaths from the group of women. David took it with honor and then smiled smugly at his friend.

Over the years, Soars with Eagles became more like a brother than Richard would ever be. He showed David how to shoot a bow. Though David never mastered it, he did hit the target several times. He, in turn, showed his friend how to shoot a shotgun. Soars with Eagles would cover his ears and grimace. David agreed—it really was too loud. Then they would both reach for their knives and have a mock knife fight, often coming out even.

David wondered how his friend was. Had the Calvary caught up with him yet? He prayed not.

As the sky began to blacken and the night creatures gathered to sing their lullabies, David stopped for the night. He tethered his two horses, Zeke and Lola, to a sturdy oak. They immediately started nibbling on the wild grasses. He set up camp under the stars—just the way he liked it. After starting a fire and eating a little something, he lay his head back on his bedroll sighing in contentment. He gazed at the sky in awe, just as he had done hundreds of times before. He lay there listening to the sounds of the night, determined to enjoy his last night on the trail alone. He would arrive in Grand Junction tomorrow. He decided to stay in town for the night before "collecting" the woman to get a good night's sleep, and harden himself that he was about to take a girl from all she had known—and deliver her to a soulless man.

TENSION

Madeline awoke to the sun peeking in through her curtains and warming her face. She smiled at the morning's eagerness to wake her, but the smile quickly fell from her lips as she realized what the day held. She groaned, then threw the covers over her head. It was a habit of hers since childhood—hiding from the world and all its little surprises...and disappointments. Her face felt tight, and her eyes swollen from crying herself to sleep.

The dreaded morning had arrived. Oh, how could she face the day? As far as she was concerned, the man coming to "collect" her was no better than the man who sent for her —and threatened her father. Her stomach bundled into a tight knot. *No breakfast today,* she thought as she forced herself from the safety of her bed. Most of her belongings were packed. She'd taken care of that last night in between fits of rage and tears of anguish. She threw everything she owned into two old trunks.

Madeline bathed herself in the quietness of her room from her pitcher and basin. She twisted her long brown hair and wrapped it tightly into a bun using a couple of pins to secure it in place. Finally, she held a cold rag on her eyes, trying to reduce their puffiness.

She heard her father greet someone at the door. Her stomach did a flip-flop. "Wonderful," she moaned, "he's here."

She had decided on traveling in her tan skirt and a white blouse, hopefully deterring the sun from taking notice of her. Here, in her beloved Colorado mountains, it got plenty warm with sunshine most of the year, but not knowing where she was heading, she thought the lighter colors would be better.

Her eyes took in every detail of her room, mentally taking pictures of what was once her sanctuary, sparse at it was. "I will not cry." She put her hand to her chest—took a deep breath and opened her door. Hesitantly, she stepped out of the shelter of her room, closing the door firmly behind her for the last time, and headed to the bright, sunlit parlor. Joseph had offered the man a cup of coffee, and both sat in awkward silence.

"Ahhh, there you are Madeline." Her father rose. "This is a... this is David. He will be your escort."

"Ma'am." David stood and tipped his head in greeting.

Madeline hardly looked at the man, but curtsied, not wanting to seem unladylike—though she did make a quick exit to the kitchen for a cup of coffee. *"Escort?"* She scoffed. She heard low murmurings from the other room—no doubt discussing her. *Oh, what were they saying?* She picked up her pace, but, of course, the murmuring stopped as soon as she returned to the room.

Joseph had warned David of Madeline's temper and stubbornness. "I fear I've neglected to harness her disposition over the years." He let out a nervous laugh. David did not smile. *What do you say in such a circumstance?* David could see the man was a sniveling coward and didn't care to engage in small talk while they waited for the young lady. He was too busy thinking to himself—*I'm almost done...freedom...*

A spark lit Madeline's eyes, perturbed at the two of them. Setting her glare on David, she said rather curtly, "You can start loading the wagon." Her arm swept towards the door. "My belongings are there, as you can see." She huffed and left the room to retrieve a remaining valise. Then, hastily tramping to the door, she peeked out, and her jaw dropped. She only saw two horses.

"Where's the wagon?"she asked.

"No wagon. Terrain's too rugged for one." He pointed to the smaller of the two horses. "You'll be ridin' Lola. She's plenty gentle and easy to guide." He was not impressed with this uptight, schoolmarm-looking woman. He had prayed for God to give him compassion for her, being as her whole world is turning upside down, but he just wanted to get on his way and be done with the whole matter.

"You can not be serious. Where are all my belongings going to go?" She scoffed, pointing to the two trunks and three bags.

Looking at all her "things" sitting by the door, David scratched his head in bewilderment. "Ma'am, all that ain't goin'. You can bring two of them little ones." He walked over to the pile, wondering which ones to pick up.

"I can not go to a new home with only *two* bags of my belongings. You will simply have to figure out a way to bring them all." One hand planted on her hip the other waving in the air, she asked, "What about a...thingy hooked up to the back of the horses, you know, one of those...thingys?"

"A travois?" *A 'thingy,' good grief.* "You can't take more

than the horses can carry," He met her obstinate gaze. "Now which two do I grab?"

She stared at him, dumbfounded for several moments. Her eyes demanded a change, but he wasn't budging. She stomped over to her things and started sorting through them, taking only what she felt she couldn't live without. She was muttering the whole time about being a lady and how this was all unfair. She grabbed a few changes of clothing, an extra pair of shoes, undergarments, her mother's brush, and mirror(which she had hidden from her father so that he couldn't sell them too), her Bible, tooth powder, a picture of her family from happier times...oh, and soap. Her eyes snapped up to her "escort." Hmmm...better throw in two of those—looks like he could use some! *What is it with cowboys and bathing?*

After attaching her two chosen valises to Lola, David pulled out a bundle from his saddlebags. *This will be interesting...* He removed his hat as he walked into the house again. "Here, Ma'am. I'd be much obliged if you'd put these on."

She took them hesitantly, then holding them up by the tips of her fingers, let out an unbelieving titter. "I don't think so...Mr...Mr..What was your name again?"

"David. Just call me David." he offered, not wanting to admit he was related to the man ripping this family apart.

"David. A lady does not wear trousers." She locked eyes with him, this time *she* refused to budge. "People will think me a wanton female."

"With all the ridin' I do believe you'll be more at ease in 'em." He attempted to explain.

"No. Thank you all the same." She handed them back to him. "I'm used to riding in a skirt." It wasn't *really* a lie. She just hadn't been riding at all in a few years since Skye was taken. With a lifting of her chin, she hastily turned around and walked to the back of the house.

"Women! This is going to be a long ride home." David mumbled to himself and started walking to the door. A hand grasped his arm, halting him. He looked down at the hand first, then turned his curious eyes on the girl's father.

"You will...take care of...of her, won't you?" The man had the gall to ask.

Gripping the man's fingers painfully in his own, he removed his hand from his arm. Joseph stifled a yelp as David got in his face and bit out, "Better than you." Then flung open the door and stormed out. David clenched and unclenched his fists. He itched to go back and pummel the man. How dare he even ask such a thing after what he was doing to his daughter. In general, David wasn't a violent man, but he had little patience for men of low character.

A few minutes later, he watched father and daughter walk out of the house, each looking pale. He knew the man was unnerved from their encounter. David saw several emotions cross over the girl's face in quick succession. Sadness, anger, dread...then resignation as she looked at her father one last time. Straightening her shoulders and tipping her chin in the air, she turned towards Lola. Frustration was evident in her tear-filled eyes. "So. How exactly am I to mount up?" David hadn't thought of that. He strolled over to her, and, before she could say another word, he grasped her waist and hoisted her up as if she weighed nothing. His lip betrayed the hint of a smile as she gaped down at him, then spun around and easily mounted his own horse. They rode in silence for a while. David was letting her have a good cry. Poor girl. Off to marry someone she's never met, leaving the only home she's ever known. *See? He could have some compassion for her.*

. . .

MADELINE TRIED her best to hold in the flood of tears, but they kept seeping out, streaming down her cheeks. *How could her father do this?* That question had plagued her over and over the last twelve hours. She feared she might never know the answer. She recalled their parting. "Father..." Madeline searched his face for any sign of remorse. But, he wouldn't even raise his eyes to look at her. "Well, goodbye..." Then, she took a deep breath and drew herself up as tall as she could and tried to force a strength she did not feel. The rest had been a blur.

Another hour passed, and David began to notice how she seemed to keep patting at her head and rubbing her temples. "Why don'tcha just take it down, no sense in tryin' to be fashionable way out here."

"A lady never lets her hair just hang down. It's improper." She tilted her head back with her nose in the air, though the pins *were* in too tightly, and added to the good-sized headache she had from trying to hold back from blubbering all afternoon.

"Darlin', there ain't nobody to see ya but me and the prairie dogs," he threw over his shoulder.

He was right, of course, but she sure wasn't going to give him the satisfaction of telling him so. "My name is Madeline, not darlin', and I've got a headache if you must know." Then she added, "Must be from the heat."

"Right...the heat." David scoffed as he guided Zeke around a rut. Madeline followed his lead as she stuck her tongue out at the back of his head. *That* was not ladylike, but it did perhaps make her feel a little better.

Some more time passed, and Madeline wished to heaven that she would have put her hair in a ponytail instead. Her head was throbbing, and the rocks and uneven path were making it unbearable.

David finally had enough. He slowed Zeke down so he was right beside a befuddled-looking Madeline. Before she knew what was happening, David yanked the two pins out of her hair and threw them to the ground.

"OW!" She yipped, reaching for her head. "I may need those!" Even in her surprise and anger, she felt immediate relief.

"Not on this trip." David tossed a piece of rawhide at her. Then he trotted up ahead.

It took everything in her not to throw the rawhide back at his curly head bobbing away! She rubbed all over her aching head, then pulled her long, straight, coffee-colored hair back into a comfortable ponytail.

4
___

WILDERNESS

M adeline had managed, somehow, to wind her way into the bramble. Getting out was another story. She had sought the seclusion of the area for some "real privacy" to relieve herself, still not trusting her companion. After she had taken care of business, she noticed her skirt caught on some thorns. She tried scooting to the left a bit, only to get snagged on that side too. She had a dilemma. The more she maneuvered, the more tangled she became. *Stupid thorns! Stupid skirt! Now what?* She paused for a minute. *If I call for help, I will never hear the end of it. If I don't, I'm likely to dig myself in deeper, then what a mess I'll be.* She huffed. *He will probably come looking for me anyway...darn it!*

David had been wondering what was taking so long when he heard a cry for help. His senses on alert, his knife in hand, he ran toward the howl. *Where was she?* "Maddie, are ya all right?"

A pitiful small voice on his right revealed the direction. "I am over here..." sniff, "I am...stuck—and my name is Madeline!" She said regaining her pride.

"Stuck?" He asked in exasperation. "Heavens, woman! I thought ya was hurt—or worse." He started slicing his way through to her. *Boy, was she a sight!* His irritation at her for causing him to worry slid away. A grin appeared on his face, and a chuckle escaped his lips.

Her temper flared. "I knew you would find this amusing! Now help me out!"

He noticed her tangled in every way possible—even her hair, which was lately drawn back into a proper ponytail, was dislodged and latched onto a branch or two. She was bent sideways to prevent it from being yanked from her head. "Guess you'll be wantin' those britches now." He offered as he worked to set her free.

"No, David. I do not. My skirt is just fine. Next time I will find a place—OUCH!" He was tugging at her hair. "Less...aggressive."

"Ma'am, ya really...are a..." He pulled and cut. "...a very stubborn woman." One more cut and she'd be free. "There!"

"Finally! Thank you." She tried to smooth her hair and straighten her skirt.

"Sure." He laughed.

"It really was not that funny." she snapped.

"Oh yes, it really was that funny." He was still struggling to master the inclination to laugh right in her face. "What I wouldn't give to've had one of those picture fellers here to capture yer likeness when I found ya."

Madeline marched off. *She knew it! She just knew he would overreact.* She could hear him laughing behind her. She bent down and grabbed a rock, then spun around, her cheeks red, ready to launch it at the snickering brute.

He stopped mid-stride and stuck his hands in the air, letting the smile drop from his lips. "All right..all right. I'll stop. Don't shoot." He clamped his mouth shut, trying to control himself. She wasn't letting go of the rock. The spark in her brown eyes remained. "Aw, come on, lady. Ya gotta ease up and learn to laugh at yerself."

He was right. Madeline had never been able to laugh at herself. She hated to be embarrassed. She began to lower her arm, and her features started to soften. She tried to hide the smile as she admitted, "I really must have looked ridiculous." She giggled. Then, they both laughed—laughed until their sides hurt.

As they traveled on, each, in turn, would start chuckling when the picture popped into their head. The much needed laughter caused some of the tension of the journey to melt away.

Another scorching day was coming to a close. The terrain was dry and dusty—desperately desiring rain. Madeline took in the breathtaking view of the mountains casting a silhouette against the pink and orange sunset. A picture only God could create. Her thoughts quickly sobered as she remembered her home in Colorado. Her beautiful, rugged San Juan mountains reached high into the heavens. Will she ever see them again? What does her future hold? She trembled at the unknown, which transported her back to thoughts of her mother. *Oh, Mama...I miss you so much. How I wish you were here. You would know just the right words to say to encourage me. I am scared, but I will try to be strong and try not to feel sorry for myself.*

Madeline's mother had attempted to teach her that life was not fair and that sometimes we have to hold fast to God and weather whatever comes our way. As she remembered such a conversation—her thoughts turned heavenward. *God, I cannot do this alone, yet I feel very alone. Help me to keep my*

*eyes on You, and face my future with dignity and the assurance of
Your presence.*

Madeline's aching muscles compelled her back to the
present. She was bone-weary from the day's ride. This trip
was very taxing on her body. She obviously was not used to
being in a saddle from sunup to sundown. She had always
enjoyed a good hour or two of the freedom she felt on the
back of Skye. But this was a very grueling pace. David
seemed to be on a time schedule and pushed them to the
limit sometimes. Madeline, on the other hand, was not in
any hurry to meet her new life. Even though she hated
sleeping outdoors, she would like to prolong the journey
indefinitely.

After about an hour more of traveling, David scouted
out a place to camp for the night.

Madeline was very eager just to lay her head down and
go to sleep...

"OHHH! I'll never be able to sleep! The ground is too hard!"
Madeline jumped up to look under her bedroll. "No wonder
—look at all these rocks. Couldn't you have found a better
place to set up camp?"

So. The bellyachin' starts. David rolled his eyes. "You are
welcome to look for another one. This ain't no fancy hotel,
ya know."

"Thank you for reminding me!" she snapped. "Speaking
of hotels...might we see one along the way?"

Just then, an eerie howling pierced the night. Madeline
scurried to where David was.

"Prairie Tenors...Coyotes." He said in a matter of
fact way.

"W...will they bother us?" Her eyes were as wide as saucers. In Colorado, she would hear them but was safe in the house, tucked in bed, with her covers over her head. Here, she was so exposed!

"Naw...we'll just keep the fire goin' all night. That'll keep 'em away," he assured her, "but, you might wanna move your bedroll closer."

She quickly grabbed it and laid it right by his.

"Not closer to me. Closer to the fire." He shook his head as he tossed on some more wood. Then he flopped down onto his back, crossed his legs, and pulled his hat over his face to get some shut-eye.

"Well, how was I supposed to know?" she said, more to herself. "Sleeping under the stars is still new to me."

Madeline heard the coyotes throughout the night. With her imagination running as wild as the animals, she pictured all kinds of horrible scenarios. In all of them, either she or David, sometimes both, wound up dead. It most certainly was not the rocky ground keeping her awake now! The last straw was when she heard some rustling in the bushes nearby. She bolted to her feet, gathered her bedroll, and moved it right between David and the fire. He was snoring away. She could not believe he could sleep through such a thing! She contemplated waking him up but decided instead to throw a few more logs on the fire—just to be sure. She got rather toasty but kept the blanket over her head anyway. After a time she fell into a deep sleep.

David was used to the outdoors with all its noises and possible dangers, so he had been sleeping soundly. What woke him up was not the coyotes; it was a hand flung over his face. He opened his eyes to see Madeline's sleeping form in front of him. Her mouth slightly open, her hair a tangle of brown partly strewn across her cheeks and forehead. "What the...?" He asked in bewilderment. He grabbed hold of her wrist and tossed it over at her. Still asleep, Madeline turned away from him over to her side.

"Women," he grumbled and fell back to sleep.

5

BATH

Waking to find herself and David in one piece, Madeline yawned and stretched, then pushed a tangle of hair out of her face. She didn't get near enough sleep, but David was up banging around, obviously trying to awaken her. She sighed, then picked herself up and headed towards the rich aroma of coffee. "Mmm-mm," she said, inhaling deeply. "Smells wonderful." Plopping down on a stump by the fire and reaching for the cup David held out for her, she asked, "So. How did you sleep?"

"Like a log," was his only reply.

THE WARMNESS of the morning spoke of the hot day ahead. They broke camp within an hour of Madeline waking. She felt sticky. She decided to keep her eyes open for a pond, lake, stream, or *something* to wash off in. Just the thought made her antsy. To take her mind off of it, she started up a conversation. "So David, tell me about yourself. I mean, we have been traveling together for a few days now, and I still don't know anything about you."

He slowed his horse so they could ride side by side. "Well...ya already know I work for Richard. But this is my last job for him. God and this line of work don't mix."

"So you're a God-fearing man."

"Yeah, you could say that." He paused. "Ya know, back a few years, I was a gamblin' man, like your Pa." He saw the surprised look on her face. "I gambled, drank, chased women." He ran a hand over his stubbled face. "Got myself into some trouble. And again, like your Pa, I became indebted to Richard. Been workin' for him ever since."

Madeline's face was downcast. She remembered her father and what brought her to this point. "What causes a man to pursue such a life? It's so destructive and...painful."

"Well to tell ya the truth, I'm not sure about yer Pa, but I didn't have much schoolin' or much direction from my folks. Gamblin' was excitin', at first, with all the money and the promise of more. Then you get sucked in. Yer in so deep you can't dig your way out. That's when men like Richard come along and make sure that you stay down. Then, he owns ya."

"How sad that there are men out there that prey on others' weaknesses." She shook her head in disgust.

"It is sad. But, because of my situation, it caused me to look up. Without desperation, I may never have found God. He's been faithful and has helped me walk upright, even in the middle of such work."

"Well, I am glad about that. You have behaved very gentlemanly...so far." She tossed a small smile towards him.

He liked her smile. "Thank you. Mabel sure would be glad to hear it."

"Who is Mabel?"

"She was our housekeeper. After my Ma and Pa died of consumption when I was young, she helped raise me," he explained.

"Oh, I'm sorry. I have heard of consumption. It's an awful sickness. I lost my Mama also," she empathized. "She and my baby brother died during childbirth."

"It's difficult to lose a parent...even one who has done ya wrong...I would guess." He threw a sidelong glance at her.

"Yes...I suppose you are right. Though I lost my father many years ago."

Madeline wasn't sure she would like anything about her new life. But, if she really allowed herself to contemplate her life so far, she wouldn't be able to see anything over the last eight years that had been good. All her best memories were from the first ten years of her life. So, this next venture was just a miserable continuation of an already pitiful existence. That is why it's best she did not dwell on it.

SQUEALING with delight and a little apprehension, Madeline ran towards the shimmering lake. The grime of the trail slid down her neck and back—her skin tingled with anticipation. Three days had passed since her last bath, and her oily hair was sticking to her scalp, screaming for a plunge in the enticing water.

Chuckling to himself at Madeline's exuberance, David led the sweat-drenched horses to a lake fed stream to cool. As they drank, he wiped them down, giving Madeline the privacy she needed to enjoy the experience fully.

Stopping at the shore, Madeline sucked in a deep breath, letting her heart calm a little as a memory surfaced. She quickly put it aside as she took in her surroundings. The oasis of trees and rocks provided all the seclusion she needed. She stripped quickly down to her chemise then eased her way into the lake, careful of her footing. The water felt amazing against her hot, aching body. The lake was calm, so she need not worry about getting swept away. "Ahhh...heaven..." She dipped her head under, relishing the coolness. Time seemed to stand still, and she was in no hurry to remind it to continue. She glided around, then flipped over to float for a while on her back—the sun caressing her as it peeked through the trees. She was perfectly content to stay in the water for the remainder of the day, and might have, had she not heard David start whistling a loud tune, reminding her he waited.

She grabbed her soap, lathered and rinsed twice to make sure all the filth was gone. Feeling completely revived, she made her way to her clothes and dressed wearing a clean gray skirt and a light blue blouse. It was nice to get out of the dirty tan skirt. She had several changes of shirts, but only two skirts, and a lovely yellow dress that reminded her of sunflowers.

"All right, David," she called, "I am decent."

As he appeared, he smiled from his dust-covered face. "Well, you look refreshed."

"Ohhh...I feel wonderful. Thank you!" and she disappeared, allowing him the same courtesy he showed her.

David was bathed and dressed within fifteen minutes.

"Just like a man," she mused, "right down to business."

"What?" he questioned as he caught her smile.

"Oh, nothing. It's just the differences between men and women are so stark."

"You can say that again." He reached for his dirty clothes so that they could have a plunge in the lake too.

"Wait! I will join you." Madeline ran to get hers as well. They took turns washing their garments with the scented soap which, at this moment, she was thankful she thought to pack. When it came to the "unmentionables," Madeline put some distance between them. David, oblivious, continued working at a coffee stain on his shirt as he whistled the same lively tune.

———

A COUPLE of days had passed since their visit to the lake, and Madeline's nose was most unhappy.

"Oh, David! Sit over there!" She pointed to a log across from her as she held her other hand over her nose. "I can't tell the difference between you and your horse."

"Excuse me, darlin', but ya ain't smellin' like a rose either." David returned as he sauntered over to the log.

Her mouth gaped open, "Why...I cannot believe you would say such a thing!" Then she turned to the side and bent down to sniff at herself. *He was right! Darn it!*

She could see the amusement on David's face and threw her most menacing scowl at him, now determined to find another lake to bathe in...for both their sakes.

THE DAYS MESHED into one another...each one seemingly hotter than the last. The sweltering sun pounded down mercilessly. Horse and human trudging forward, not an inch dry anywhere on them from all the fluid seeping from their bodies. David and Madeline had walked the last couple of hours trying to save the horse's strength. They had started the day with plenty of water. Now, he feared running dry before nightfall blanketed the land in coolness, and they could replenish their supply.

David tried to avoid as much of the Great Desert as possible, but it was too massive to go around. He picked the best route through it that he could—one that he had done many times before, but only with himself and Zeke to worry about. He knew that if they kept on this path slightly heading northwest, they should encounter several small streams and rivers once they enter into Nevada. The Great Basin would not be a picnic either, but at least they'd have more access to water and shelter.

Hearing a moan behind him, David turned to see Madeline lying in a heap, Lola close by. He rushed to her side and gently rolled her over. Her eyes were closed; her parched mouth was open. Jogging back to Zeke, he pulled his canteen out and a chunk of salt and ran back to her. He slowly poured the liquid down her throat. Then, wetting the salt rock, wiped some over her cracked lips. He kept repeating the process until Madeline's surprised eyes fluttered open. "Wh...what happened?" She attempted to push herself up onto her elbows. David assisted her into a sitting position as he explained her collapse. He was still concerned for her; she looked incredibly red-faced and confused. He feared heat exhaustion. What she needed was shade, rest, and lots of water.

David practically pushed her up on Lola. She tried to protest that she was fine and that Lola didn't need the added burden. But, it fell on deaf ears. He thrust his hat on her head and handed her his canteen. "Drink. Small continuous sips." He then placed the reins in her free hand. "Now hold on...don't be fallin' off and squashin' my hat." He gave her a wry grin. "We have got to get you out of this heat."

An hour or so further, they and the horses wholly drained of liquid and energy, David made camp by a little stream. He first helped Madeline down by the water, which she practically fell into trying to get at the desired refreshment. Then, he led the horses downstream to take their fill. He then stumbled over to Madeline and dropped to his knees, then lay on his belly and slurped up as much as he could handle. Taking handfuls of water, he splashed it over and over onto his head and face. Turning onto his back, all strength gone, he dropped his head toward Madeline. She looked like a drowned cat. "You feelin' better?" He chuckled. She smiled tentatively before collapsing onto her back. Both were content just to lay by the stream and take a much-needed nap before attempting to do anything else. When the sun went down, after David had rustled up a little something for them to eat, both sat in exhausted silence by the light of a small crackling fire, each continuing at times to put cold rags on their sunburned faces. Then, they both drifted off into uninterrupted sleep—only to rise the next day to do it all again and again...

6

RAIN

They smelled the rain coming. The dark, ominous clouds threatened to unleash their fury. Flashes of lightning illuminated an outcropping of trees and rocks ahead. The low rumble of thunder seemed to move the ground beneath them. David knew they had to find shelter quickly. The trees up ahead looked promising. They urged their mounts into a gallop. It was a race against the approaching storm. The question was—who would win?

The drops of rain came softly at first, washing away the day's dust and heat. But, the closer they got to the trees, the harder the rain came, slapping against their cheeks and blurring their vision, making it harder to discern where they were heading. They had lost the race. The sky held nothing back; the dry, parched land couldn't swallow the rain fast enough. Lightning streaked from the heavens all around, threatening to engulf them.

By the time they reached the covering, not a spot on them was dry. They slowed their pace as they wound their way through, hoping to find a cave of some sort to take refuge inside. The trees were not sheltering them from the elements as much as they had hoped, plus they seemed to be a target for the lightning.

David rapidly glanced about. He had been in the area before; if he could just find the rock formation...there it was! They made their way to it just as lightning struck a tree behind them.

The lightning was worse than Madeline had ever seen before in her life. She was terrified. Back home during a storm, of course, she would hide her head under the covers. Then, she would hum a tune trying to block out the menacing thunder that jarred her teeth.

They made it to a wide-mouth cave, not very deep, but tall enough for the horses to take shelter in also. They quickly dismounted and tethered the horses between two rocks. There wasn't much light except for when the sky lit up. At those times, David rushed around looking for wood to build a fire. They desperately needed the heat to dry themselves and their blankets. Madeline was shivering so much her teeth chattered. David worked and worked to get a small fire going that he could build on, but he was dripping wet and kept putting out whatever started. He jumped up and threw his hat to the side, rolled up his sleeves, and squeezed the water from his hair. Then, he tried again. Finally! After he had a constant flame, he put everything he could on it until it blazed.

"Maddie, see if ya can find anything drier to wear, then search my things for somethin' for me to put on," he stood to leave. "I have to get more wood so we have enough to last us."

"But won't it be wet?" she asked.

"Yep," he said, then went out into a horizontal sheet of rain.

"Well, Lola...that does not make any sense to me, does it

to you?" She was pulling at her valise with chilled fingers. Her breath came in quick bursts from being so cold. "You either, huh, Zeke?... Did he just call me Maddie again?"

Everything on top was soaked, but she did find her white cotton nightgown was only a little damp. She fumbled with the buttons on her shirt to the point of almost just ripping it off—she was so frustrated.

David made an appearance with arms full of wood, then left again. Thunder boomed, making her squeal and jump. She threw her clothes in the direction of the fire, then headed to Zeke in hunt for David's clothes. In his satchel, she found a pair of long johns that were partially dry. She hurried over to the fire. "My, won't we be a pair," she commented as she spread out her clothes and their blankets to dry.

David stumbled in again dropping the wood in a pile. "I like what you've done with the place," he smiled, then headed out again.

Both horses appeared unsettled from the storm. "I know how you feel." Madeline lightly patted their necks to calm them. Then, twisting abruptly, "Oh! I know what he is doing. He thinks the fire will help dry the wood! Clever man...no telling how long we will be here." She jumped up to do her part by stacking the wood in a way best to dry, while David made a few more trips.

By the time David finished, he was a sopping, dripping mess—and he was freezing. First things first, he had to get out of those clothes.

"Ma...Maddie..." his teeth clanked. "I...ne..need yer...help." She rushed over to him. "Mm..my shirt."

"Oh, David. You are like ice!" She took hold of his shirt and started working at the buttons. She was sure if she could see his lips, they would be blue. Without a second thought, she unfastened his belt and pants for him. She would have continued to help him out of them, but he stopped her. "O..OK...I can d..do it. Thank...y...you."

This wasn't a time for modesty. She was worried about him. But, she backed away, respecting his wishes. She went over to check on the blankets. They were too wet to do any good. Still chilled, she hunched down by the fire pulling her knees to her chest.

The rain was coming down in torrents. The lightning and thunder continued into the night. They huddled close to each other for body warmth—more for David's sake, who was still shaking. It took a good while before they felt toasty. Every once in a while, Madeline would rise to turn their blankets and clothing.

The noise of the tempest was too unsettling to Madeline's ears, so to distract herself, she asked, "I noticed your knife sheath on your belt. It is remarkable. Where did you get it?"

David loved the topic of his Cheyenne friends and talked about them and Soars with Eagles over the next hour.

Madeline was fascinated by the stories. She encouraged him to continue, even though he began to yawn and grow heavy-eyed. He shared all of his and Soars with Eagles exploits with the US Cavalry. After a while, she finally let David stop and get some sleep. That night, she dreamed about the barely clad warriors chasing buffalo...

THE STORM SHOWED no sign of letting up. David had wanted to go try to find something for them to eat, but Madeline wouldn't hear of him going out and getting soaked again. They had plenty of bouillon and rainwater to last them. Bouillon didn't have much substance to it, so she knew his stomach must have been unsatisfied. He usually tried to add some meat to it.

She got up and started rummaging through their supplies. "There has to be some... Ha!" At the bottom of the bag, she found a rag tied around a lump of dried apples. "Here," she thrust the open rag at him. "This should help."

"Where in the world did you find that? I looked all over." He grabbed for it.

"Well, obviously not all over," she teased him. "I found it at the bottom of the bag. Now eat! I'm tired of hearing your stomach growl."

MADELINE WAS thankful to have her Bible with her. To help pass the time, she read some Scriptures from the book of Psalms, which was her favorite.

During this time, she discovered that David couldn't read or write well. His parents never put a strong emphasis on schooling, and, being a boy who would rather be outdoors fishing, hunting, and riding, he wasn't motivated himself.

David wasn't embarrassed about it—never felt like he missed out on anything. He memorized Scriptures whenever he heard them. He may not have been able to read well, but his memory was incredible. But while here in the cave with Maddie, he let her try to teach him. She seemed to come alive, and her eyes would dance in the firelight whenever he succeeded at a word. He liked seeing her smile.

THEY ENDED up staying for two days before the sun broke through the clouds. Everything smelled fresh and clean. As they emerged, the vivid colors of the landscape, crystallized by the sparkling raindrops, ensnared Madeline's keen eyes. "Beautiful." She took a deep breath and slowly released it. "It's at times like this, I know God is real. It has His signature all over it." David readily agreed.

It wasn't a bath, but Madeline had to admit, she felt cleaner and smelled a little better after the good soaking. They had lost some time, but both felt recuperated from the many days traveling. The horses were sure glad to be free of their prison. David sent them off running to work their legs before they got underway again. At his whistle, both came trotting back.

7

TOWN

After another week on the trail, one bath, and many hot, blistering days, Madeline couldn't believe her ears. David informed her that they would soon be coming up on the one and only town on their trip. And, that they would be staying a couple of nights to rest the horses.

"A town? Really...truly?" She could barely contain herself.

"Yep."

"A real bath? A real bed...real food...and...people?" She squealed with delight.

"Yep, real people."

"Oh, David. I didn't mean it like that. It is just that it has only been you and me for so long, it will be nice to talk to some other people, that is all." She cast him a look. "Don't pout, really David."

He enjoyed seeing her squirm. He was actually looking forward to the short visit. He knew some people in the saloon there. Most knew of his changed life, and, though they didn't understand it, they accepted him as long as he didn't "preach at 'em."

Several days ago, they were laid up in the cave. Since then, they had traveled hard. David wanted to get back on schedule but knew Madeline needed some pampering. He was impressed at how well she adapted to the riding, sleeping outdoors, and the few and far between baths. At first, he didn't think either one of them would make it. He was tempted to leave her in the wild a time or two when she whined or nagged him too much. But so far, both of them had survived each other, and he wanted to reward her. Plus, he needed a break from her constant yammerin'. It may be awful to think, but he sure missed the quiet, solitude before she came along. Don't get him wrong, he also took pleasure in her company. At first, she seemed high-falutin', with all her prim and proper talk and mannerisms, but he since discovered that a lot of it was just a put on. Deep down, she was a scared, insecure little girl who hated her father and needed her mother desperately. He pitied her, which also made the desire to protect her rise up in him. Yep, both of them needed this reprieve from the trail.

The traffic of people picked up considerably the closer they drew to the town. Many were in covered wagons, which looked like a heavenly way to travel compared to what Madeline had been through in the saddle. She wished she looked more presentable; what they must think of her! David didn't seem to mind one way or another, which irritated her. She knew she just needed a nice, warm bath and a comfortable bed.

The last few miles seemed endless to Madeline. *Oh that he would not have even mentioned the town until they were upon it!* The saddle seemed unbearable now. It would have probably been fine had she not known what was ahead. But she did! And she couldn't stand it any longer. She urged Lola to a trot and threatened a gallop, but David stopped her.

"No sense gettin' yer dander up. We'll be there soon enough. You don't wanna spook the other travelers, now do ya?" He wanted to get there too. She was making him stir crazy with all her fidgeting and moaning and carrying on. He did trot alongside her until they came to the town entrance. Then, they both walked their horses calmly, to "Red Mary's Saloon and Hotel."

David could tell Madeline wasn't so sure of the place. Granted, it wasn't anything fancy, but it was a suitable stay. She'd get her bath and nice, comfy bed. Besides, it wasn't one of Richard's establishments, and David was grateful for that fact. He just wanted a little R&R. No business dealings.

He secured a couple of rooms for them and asked if someone could show Madeline to hers. "I've got catchin' up to do."

With that, Madeline watched as he sauntered over to the bar where a buxom red-headed lady was tending. "Oh I bet." she said under her breath as she followed a boy up the stairs. She stared at David as she ascended.

He was leaning on the counter with one knee bent and a foot propped on a low ridge off the floor. He tipped his hat back on his head as he chuckled at something the redhead said. Madeline felt the heat rising to her cheeks. As if sensing she was watching him, David casually lifted his eyes to meet hers. She saw the merriment dancing in them. She quickly turned her head, and, wouldn't you know it—she tripped on her skirt! The heat rose even further from embarrassment. She dared not look at him again, but picked up her skirt and flung herself up the rest of the stairs. She quickly dismissed the service boy and slammed the door behind her. Pressing her back to it, she scolded herself. Why wasn't she more careful? How could she face him after that humiliation? And, why did she feel a tinge of jealousy as she watched him laughing with that woman? It bothered her that she cared. Though she was quite famished, she could not show her face downstairs tonight.

Madeline couldn't keep herself from playing the incident over and over in her mind as she bathed. She tried to enjoy the warmth of the liquid sloshing over her, but her tormenting mind wouldn't allow it. *What was David doing now? Was he enjoying Red Mary's company? Or some other woman's?* The thought disgusted her and, at the same time, brought a pang of envy. *What am I thinking? I don't care about David! He can be with whoever he wishes!*

Only after the water became cold did she have a reprieve from her thoughts. She dried and dressed herself, then climbed into the soft bed. She was savoring the feel of something other than a hard ground, when hunger pangs struck, reminding her of why she hadn't eaten. Then the thoughts started up again. Late into the night she tossed and turned in agony. It wasn't supposed to be like this! She was looking forward to her bath, a meal, talking with some of the locals, and she was supposed to be enjoying this bed! She was free from sticks and stones poking at her through the bedroll, but her mind was suffering far worse than her body ever did.

MADELINE AWOKE to a pounding on her door. Startled out of her wits and groggy from a restless night, she hobbled to the door. "Who is it?"

"It's me," she heard David's voice. "I was wonderin' if you were gonna ever come down and eat some breakfast."

She let out a sigh as her stomach grumbled. "Ah...give me a few minutes."

"Sure. I'll see ya downstairs." She heard his boots echo down the hall.

Rubbing her tired eyes, she made her way to the washbasin. Pushing her matted hair away, she splashed the cool water onto her face. "Brrrrr...if that doesn't wake me up, I am not sure anything will!"

Picking up her mirror, she groaned at the image staring back at her. "Ugh. I'm not fit to see anybody." Her face was brown from all the time on the trail. Gone was her perfect, white porcelain skin. She even noticed freckles! Nobody could ever find her attractive with those all over her! She sighed and began the tedious job of combing out her tangled hair. "Humph. That's a little better." Today, she decided to look like a civilized lady and wear her yellow dress, which was one of her favorites. "I wonder what David will think of this..." Then, shaking her head as if to clear it, "What on earth made me say that?"

She put her hair up in a loose bun, leaving some strands dangling down, and pulled a few wisps down around her face. "Ahhhh...now that's better," she said, admiring herself in the large dresser mirror.

Feeling very feminine, she twirled her way to the door. Ignoring the voice inside screaming, "Remember yesterday? You made a fool of yourself!" she was determined to make the most of this day in town... with or without David.

"My, my, Maddie. You look as fresh as a nice spring day." He bowed to her, and she curtsied in return. He had to admit, her sun-kissed cheeks, with a sprinkle of freckles draped across them, looked very becoming. Much better than that pale, sickly look she had when they first met.

Blushing slightly, she said, "Why thank you, David. You

clean up nicely yourself." His bronzed face was cleanly shaved, and his teeth sparkled as he grinned. He was wearing a light green shirt she had never seen before. He was rather fine-looking this morning.

After eating a filling breakfast of biscuits and gravy, sausage, and eggs, they took a stroll around the town taking in all there was to see. David gave her some money to buy a few items, while he went to the stables to check on the two horses.

Madeline found a beautiful, soft, green nightgown made of an exquisite satin. She loved the feel of it against her cheek. She decided she just had to have it. It would take most of the money David gave her, but it was too beautiful to pass up. After weeks in the saddle without any luxuries, she felt she was due some comfort. The coloring reminded her of David's shirt. Of course, it would be for the wedding night...to...Richard. She quickly paid for it before she changed her mind. She also bought a simple, brown barrette to replace the rawhide when they arrived at Belle Rive, some stockings, and a simple light blue dress for more everyday wear.

With her money spent, she met David outside. They made their way back to Red Mary's Saloon and enjoyed a not so quiet dinner. The locals were gathering for cards and drinks, but David and Madeline didn't mind. The food was wonderful, and they were enjoying each other's company.

David never did bring up her stumble up the stairs, or her behavior after. For that she was very thankful. And in return, Madeline didn't bring up his flirting with the voluptuous redhead, Mary. Though, the more Madeline learned of his character, the more she doubted that David was anything other than honorable.

After another nice, hot, soothing bath, Madeline slept

peacefully that night. She wasn't looking forward to the morning and leaving this little bit of heaven.

Now it was David's turn to toss and turn. He couldn't stop thinking about Maddie and the way she looked that day. Beauty radiated out of her. The soft way her hair framed her face, and the pale yellow dress that hung a little loose on her small frame after some time of improper eating on the trail, her brown eyes sparkling in merriment as they took in the town...the urge to protect her, especially from Richard, began to wind and tangle itself in his mind...and his heart.

THE NEXT MORNING as they bid farewell to the comforts of the town, each was left with their own thoughts. Any chit-chat felt forced and uncomfortable. Feelings that they hadn't expected started to surface, but both were unwilling to explore them.

The cloud-infested sky, as it released tiny pellets of rain, promised cooler traveling. The weather seemed very much like the turmoil churning in their minds.

8

RIVER

Madeline wasn't sure which was worse. The pounding of the unrelenting sun, or the constant days of steady rain? Both were miserable! Lately, their supplies were always wet when they stopped for the night. The wood was wet, the ground was wet; it's no wonder she had a sniffle. Then today, the sun came back with a vengeance.

They could hear the roar of the river a ways off. The rain over the last couple of days had turned the once gently flowing river into a force to be reckoned with.

When they reached it, David took off his stetson wiping the sweat from his brow, then slapped his hat against his thigh. There was no way they could cross here. They'd have to look for an easier spot. He turned to Madeline. "We'll follow along the river a while and see if we can cross further down." He clicked his heels under Zeke and pulled the reins to turn him south.

About a half mile down they found an area. The water was still high but looked a bit calmer. David took notice of a tree lodged against some rocks in the middle. Yanking Zeke around, he stopped in front of Madeline. "All right. This is where we cross. I'll lead to make sure of the footin' and see how deep it is. We'll cross up a ways from that tree." He pointed to the area. "We'll try to avoid the strongest current, but nothin's for certain."

He noticed the look of concern etched across her features. "Maddie, it'll be fine. Just follow me. There are underwater currents we have to be careful of, but Lola is strong. She'll get ya through." *Was she listening?*

The moment she dreaded was upon her. Madeline was terrified of the river. She had nearly drowned when she was a child in the river by her home. Her foot slipped off the rocks she had been playing on, and she plunged into the swift moving water. At the time, she didn't have a healthy respect for the power of the river. She did now. David was talking to her, something about 'follow and currents,' but she couldn't hear him. She was too wrapped up in the turbulent waters in front of her.

"Madeline!" he yelled. That got her attention. He never called her Madeline. She looked his way and licked her lips out of nervousness. "Maddie, ya gotta listen...follow me. Keep yer eyes on my back. Don't look at the water; focus on me. Do you understand?" He was getting a little worried. She looked downright scared.

"Follow you...look at you...got it." She tried a half smile.

He paused, not sure what to do. They had to cross the river. There was no other way. "All right." He touched Madeline's clenched hand to reassure her. "Watch me. Here we go." He lead Zeke slowly into the water. "On Zeke...easy boy." He made sure Maddie was following, then trudged on. He'd have to keep his eyes on the task at hand and abstain from looking back at her or they both could end up in a lot of trouble.

He could feel the tug of the water the further they went in. Zeke stumbled a bit. "Steady boy...easy does it." The sound of the river was deafening in his ears. He prayed Maddie would be all right. He wouldn't know until he reached the other side. He directed Zeke slightly upstream to avoid the rocks and tree, knowing certain calamity would overtake them if they got too close.

Madeline tried hard to focus on the blue of David's shirt. "Just watch him...follow him...you can do this..." Lola lost her footing, which caused Madeline to panic. She looked into the pool of swirling, angry water. "No...I can't do this! David!" she screamed, but it was swallowed up by the roaring of the water. She hadn't noticed that he had veered upstream and she was being pulled in the direction of the rocks. She suddenly felt a tug on her skirt. "On Lola! Please GO!" She was stuck. As she turned to see what she was caught on, Lola lurched forward trying to get her footing back and fight the onslaught of the rushing river. Madeline lost her balance and was flung into the churning waters. "DAAV..." Her head dipped under. Her skirt was tangled on the tree branches, and she was wedged against the rocks. The force of the river was so strong she couldn't break free. She fought with every ounce of energy to keep her head up, which was proving more and more difficult with each passing second. "Oh God...help...," she gurgled, "...me!"

David had made it to the other bank and quickly turned to make sure Maddie was close behind him. He saw Lola surging toward the bank, but no Maddie. His eyes frantically searched for her. "Dear God...Maaaaddieeee!" Yelling was useless; he could barely even hear himself. There! He saw her! She was caught in the current, pinned to the rocks, her skirt clearly caught on the tree. His thoughts ran as wild as the river. What should he do? He fought the urge to jump to her rescue, knowing the river was too powerful for him. He had to use his brain. "Think, David! Think!" Quickly he grabbed a rope from Zeke's saddle and ran upstream a ways. He tied the rope to a large tree, making sure it was secure. Then, looped it around his waist and knotted it. He ran back to Zeke, jumped in the saddle, and they plunged into the river. He couldn't take a chance at being careless or horse and rider would be lost. "Easy boy...easy...steady as she goes." His adrenaline at full peak, he kept Zeke on pace.

He had almost reached her. "Hang on..." Her head was barely above the water, and she was being slammed by the rapids. He slid off Zeke into the lurking mass and hit the rocks to the side of her. First, he tried to raise her up so her head would be completely above water. Then, he attempted to pull her to him, fighting the current. She would budge a little, but her skirt being tangled in the branches wouldn't allow her freedom. He would have to thrust himself over her to unhook it. Every muscle in his body struggled with the heavy force beating against him. "GRRAAWWW!" he roared as he propelled himself around her. He grabbed at the skirt and yanked as hard as he could. Finally! It broke free. Turning back, he reached for her and pulled her to him. She wrapped her arms around his neck. "Hold on!" he yelled in her ear. "Don't let go!"

Though the force of the river held her against him, it would be that same force he would have to contend with to pull them to safety. He was getting tired, but he could not...would not let her go. "Give me strength, God..." he said through clenched teeth. Zeke was about five yards away, planted like an oak weathering a storm. "If I ...can...just make...it to...him..." David fought and fought. Pulled and pulled. Just when his strength was spent and he couldn't take it anymore, they made it to Zeke. Reaching out, he grabbed onto the cincha underneath the horse, and with as much gusto as he could muster, yelled, "Go Zeke!" The horse did the rest of the work for him—going against the unrelenting current, he pulled them to safety. David had trouble letting go of the horse. His hand was in a vice grip. Madeline was spitting and sputtering as she attempted to catch her breath. Willing his fingers loose, he grabbed for her and started beating on her back to help get the water from her lungs. Then, they both collapsed onto their backs, exhausted and with labored breath. Neither spoke for a long time.

It was Madeline who broke the silence. "David..." His head rolled to the side to face her. "Thank you...thank you for saving my life." She got a little choked up, and a tear escaped.

He raised his hand to gently wipe away the lone tear. "Thank God yer alright..."

She laid hold of his hand and held it against her cheek, relishing the strength of it.

Though their progress would be cut short for the day, they decided the horses, not to mention themselves, deserved to rest. They found a spot close to the river to set up camp for the night.

9

SKIRT

Wringing out her river-drenched hair, Madeline watched David begin to build a fire. His wet shirt was clinging to him, outlining the muscles underneath. She was fascinated with their movement. He turned towards her, which caused her to blush a little and turn away.

One side of his mouth curled up with the hint of a smile. "After I get the water out of my clothes, I'll find us somethin' to eat."

"Oh...all right." she said nonchalantly and began to comb her fingers through her long locks. It was a tangled mess from her bout in the river. She heard the crackle of the fire, which made her body break out in goose bumps from the wet clothes she was still wearing. She turned toward the flames and attempted to stand when her eyes caught sight of David shirtless. *Oh my...* She continued to stare at his bare chest and finely tuned muscles as he squeezed the water out of his shirt. She had never seen a bare-chested man before, and, she had to admit, she liked what she saw! Her heart began to beat a little faster and heat rose into her cheeks.

His light brown curls, appearing darker and longer from the water, danced in the sunlight.

She realized she was gawking at him and quickly averted her eyes, taking a couple of deep breaths to slow her wildly beating heart. He was a very handsome man, now that she allowed herself to think about it. She giggled to herself, then went on to put her hair into a quick braid.

David thought he saw, let's call it "appreciation" on Maddie's face when he caught her looking at him. It made his insides warm to have her eyes on him. *Ach! What am I thinkin'? I can't allow myself to have those thoughts! She is to be another man's wife, and I am to be...a godly man.* He threw on his damp shirt, leaving it unbuttoned, and walked over to their bundles. After fidgeting with the buckles, he pulled out the "dreaded" britches. *This should cool things down a bit.* Then, with a look of determination, he swaggered over to where Maddie was sitting. She turned toward him with a smile, then let it drop off her face like melted wax when she saw what he was holding.

"Here, put these on. They're dry." He plopped them on to her lap.

Shaking her head, she said, "I don't think so."

He couldn't believe that *even now*, she refused. "Look Maddie, after all the trouble that thing has caused, don'tcha think you oughta listen to me and wear the britches?" He tried to reason with her but was starting to get a little testy.

"No. I do not." Head tilted up and lips pursed, she glared at him. "And I thought we had already been through all this."

"Well, I for one have had it with that...that female contraption. Either ya take it off or I will!" he warned and started to walk away.

"Oh, you wouldn't dare!" She stood with her hands rooted on her hips.

He slowly turned back to her, eyebrows arched and head tilted down with a self-assured look on his face. He had accepted her challenge and started to close the gap between them.

Her eyes widened, and she stumbled backwards trying to get away. Then, her *stupid* skirt caught on a broken limb. She pulled at it frantically, but it wouldn't let loose.

David caught one of her wrists and held firmly, then with the other hand, reached around her waist and deftly unbuttoned her skirt. She tried swatting at him with her free hand, but he dodged her attempts and swiftly ensnared her flailing hand and tucked it in his grip with the other wrist. As the skirt fell to the ground in a crumble, he reached for her petticoat, pausing to see if she would relent.

Tears of embarrassment threatened to escape. "All right...ALL RIGHT! Stop! I'll change into the trousers."

He looked into her waterlogged, angry eyes, "You promise?"

"Yes!...just let me go." She looked like a whipped child. Her pride that was hurt than anything else.

As soon as he released her, she yanked up the trousers and stormed off into the trees for cover. "And don't you dare look!"

"Don't worry. I won't!" he yelled back. "Females!" He scooped up the "bone of contention" and tossed it on top of the fire pit. Then, added kindling and more wood to make sure it burned. It was smoking something awful because of the wetness, but he was determined it not exist to see another day.

"There. You satisfied?" Madeline was attempting to put some rope into the belt loops to hold up the pants. "What is that sm..." She gasped, gawking wide-eyed at the smoke rising from the fire pit. "Is that my...that's my skirt! *Why did you do that?*"

"Just in case ya got the notion to put it back on." He noticed how she had to hold the pants up to keep them from falling and smiled. "Need some help with those too?"

Her eyes smoldered. Fuming, she stalked away.

Maddie didn't talk to him for the rest of the night, which was fine with him. He was busy mapping out the rest of their trek in his head. He had caught some fish for their dinner earlier, and Maddie was busy frying it up and making some coffee.

When the sun dipped behind the hills, the night began to chill. Though she shivered, she refused to sit anywhere near him, and he was by the fire.

"*Stubborn woman!*" he thought as he ate a second helping.

When she finished eating, she took the plates and cups to the river to wash them. It was such a beautiful evening. Thousands of stars were winking down at her; the moon cast a soft glow on the gently rolling landscape. She sighed as she realized it was all wasted on her and her sour mood. "I know what You are thinking God... I am a rebellious, willful child. *But what about him?* Did You see what he did to my skirt?" She paused, "Not to mention my pride...I mean, really!"

She didn't stop to listen, maybe knowing what He would whisper to her heart if she did. Instead, she stomped back to camp, laid out her bedroll, and crawled underneath her blanket. "*Chilly night,*" she thought, and curled up like a baby, making sure her back was facing *him*.

She was exhausted from her adventure in the river, but, for a couple of hours, lay awake listening to the cracking

and sputtering of the fire. She also could hear David's soft
voice humming a tune she didn't recognize. *Oh, why did she
have to fight him so?* If she got down to the crux of it, she
knew she was starting to feel for him in a way not allowed to
her. She was to marry another man...*Oh*...her thoughts were
interrupted. Hearing footsteps approaching, she feigned
sleep.

David bent down and spread another blanket over her
small form. Sitting on his haunches, he just stayed there,
looking at her for a few minutes. He finally bent his head
and whispered a prayer.

"Father, you've entrusted this woman into my
care...Why? I haven't figured that out yet. But help me to do
right by her...and maybe help her to be a little more coop-
erative."

With that, he rose up and threw more wood on the fire to
keep the animals away. Then he went to lay on his bedroll.

Other than the *last* part, Madeline's heart began to
soften at his words. He prayed for her! No one had done that
since her mother. The thought caused a warm tear to trickle
down across the bridge of her nose. The more she got to
know him, the more she admired him. Well—most of the
time, when he wasn't making her angry or driving her crazy.
That made her smile. She knew he had used his own
blanket to cover her—they had no other. With those sweet
thoughts, before she knew it she drifted into a dreamless
sleep.

10

SNAKE

Barely light out, David awakened to the sound of some rustling and slightly audible shrieks coming from his left. He lifted up on one arm, and, with the other, ran his hand over his whiskered face, then through his sleep-flattened curls. *"What in the world is she doing now?"* he grumbled to himself as he watched her wield a large stick and strike the ground.

"Maddie...what are you doin'?" he asked through a yawn.

"Nothing...I can't..." she hit at the ground again, "handle!" Another muffled scream escaped. Pounding hard, "Oh, I got you...you...you slithering, nasty thing!" Then, she lurched backward and tripped on a rock.

David was on his feet when he heard the sound of rattling. *Naw...she couldn't be!* Like lightning, he drew his knife and let it sail through the air impaling the snake to the ground as it lunged at her.

She lifted herself up, dusting off. "I told you I could handle it!" she shouted.

"Oh...oh really? And your *handling* it was to hit it with a *stick?*" he yelled back. "Use common sense woman...it coulda bit ya!"

Her voice still raised, "Well, you were over there snoring like ole' Rip Van Winkle. What was I supposed to do?"

"*Who?* And that's beside the point. Ya shoulda woken me!" They were standing close now.

"I would have..."

Without warning, he grabbed her by the waist and kissed her quiet. At first, her hands went to his chest to push back, but then found her arms slipping up around his neck melting into his embrace, returning the kiss. He tugged her closer, then with a sudden jolt of conscience, he broke the kiss, dropping his arms and stepping back simultaneously. "I...a...I'm sorry Maddie. I shouldn't have done that."

Flustered, he turned and walked away. He quickly withdrew his knife, wiping the blade in the grass, and yanked up the snake. Then, swaggered over to the fire pit. "So...I guess rattlesnake is on the menu."

Standing there, weak-kneed and stunned, Madeline lifted her hand to her quivering lips. They felt warmed by his kiss. She was a little ashamed of what she was thinking...*Why did he have to stop?* Never having been kissed by a man, she didn't know what to do with herself, so she began to roll up her sleeping mat. Then, something popped into her mind. Did he say we're eating *snake* for breakfast?

David was angry with himself for not showing more control. It just...happened...and he enjoyed it...a little too much. *What was he thinking?*

He gutted the snake and skewered it with a stick, then put it over the fire to sizzle. Meanwhile, Madeline cleaned up and prepared the coffee. An uncomfortable silence ensued.

After getting over the initial disgust at eating snake,

Madeline surprised them both at how much she ate...and how much she enjoyed it.

BOTH WERE VERY sore from their incident in the river yesterday. The movement of the horses caused every muscle to make its presence known.

The day was much hotter than the previous days. Madeline was thankful they were able to fill up their canteens in the river before departing. The liquid was leaving in drops of sweat as fast as she was putting it in. She tried to cover herself the best she could to keep her skin from baking in the unrelenting rays. Even the horses were struggling. What she wouldn't do for some of that rain from a few days ago. At one point, she thought she was going to pass out. She then decided the heat of the sun was definitely worse than days of rain.

There wasn't much in the way of covering around, but they took refuge in whatever they could find. It wouldn't do any good to push on. They would travel more when the sun went down. For now, they did their best to cool off.

ALTHOUGH THE SUN HAD RECEDED, the earth was radiating its heat. They had commenced riding. David hoped to get in a few hours before stopping again. Even the breeze was warm.

When they finally did stop for the night, though zapped from the sweltering heat of the day, they both had a fitful sleep—each thinking about the kiss and how much they were starting to care for the other.

11

TAKEN

Dreading the day ahead because of his lack of sleep but wanting to get an early start, David pulled himself from his thoughts and his bedroll before the sun began to peek over the horizon. The warmth of the night spoke of the blistering day ahead. They would travel until the sun was directly overhead, then break until it started to dip down below the hills. They would then ride into the dark of night, sleep for a few hours, and start all over again.

He felt he could handle the heat of the day much more so than Maddie. She had looked as if she might topple off her mount yesterday from heat exhaustion. Of course, she would never admit it...stubborn woman! She wasn't about to give in and own up to the fact that she needed to rest or needed his help.

Now as he began to pack up camp, he glanced over at her sleeping form, her face tinged red from the sun. She looked so peaceful...angelic...even vulnerable. *"Don't let it fool ya, David."* he muttered to himself. *"She's far from it!"*

"Ahem." He broke the silence of the morning. "Rise and shine, Maddie...gotta get ahead of the sun."

"Ohhhhh," she groaned. "It can't be time to go...I feel as if I just fell asleep." She struggled to open her eyes. "It's still dark."

"Yeah, but it'll be light soon enough. I think we're in for another scorcher. Best to get movin' early." he explained.

"Oh, great. Another hot day." She threw the cover up over her head.

"Come on, getta wiggle on," he said as he nudged her with his boot. "We're breakin' camp in half an hour."

Madeline slowly lifted herself to a sitting position. Her mouth felt dry, and her face and hands felt sticky. Her brown hair obviously tried to escape the quick braid she threw it in last night. She rubbed her grit-filled eyes and gave a huge yawn. Then, standing, she reached for the heavens, wincing as she stretched her tight, aching muscles.

This journey was taking a toll on her body, not to mention her spirits. The closer they got to their destination, the more foreboding crept into her heart. She was at odds with herself. Part of her wished to be done with this grueling trip. The other part dreaded what awaited her at its end.

She turned her back to David, attempting to make herself more presentable. "*I must look dreadful,*" she thought as she walked into the trees for some "privacy."

When she returned, David was pouring some coffee. "Would you like a cup?"

"Ohhh, yes...thank you." She clumsily plopped down next to the fire. His fingers brushed hers as he handed her the cup. She felt her face flush and her insides warm. She quickly took a sip to try to hide how his touch affected her.

Clearing his throat, he asked if she'd like some of the

stew he had warmed up. He was uncomfortable with the way he responded to her nearness. His attraction for her had been building, but now...

Over to the left, a horse's snort got his attention. He swiftly rose to his feet which slightly alarmed Madeline.

The streaks of the morning light began to illuminate his surroundings. His eyes fell on a form by the tree cropping. He heard a gun click...then saw three men emerge from the shadows, each holding a gun pointed in his direction.

Quickly, he drew Maddie to him, spilling her coffee down the front of her blouse, and tucked her behind him protectively. Her heart was pounding as she saw the three men move in closer. She felt David's muscles stiffen—his hand gripping at his sheath.

"Mr. Shelton...David...and how are ya this fine mornin'?" the man in the middle rasped. "Ma'am." He tipped his hat to Madeline.

Mr. Shelton? Madeline took note.

"McCreedy." David said through clenched teeth. "What do you want? Why all the guns?"

"Well now, Davey," McCreedy started. "Seems yer brother has short-changed us from our last col-lection. He owes us ten pieces of silver each. Ain't that right, boys?"

Brother...Madeline reflected as the truth dawned on her.

"Yep." The other two spoke in unison. David recognized them as Doogan and Roy.

"Yer barkin' at a knot. What's that got to do with me?" David asked. "Take it up with Richard."

"Problem is..." McCreedy paused, "is that Richie boy don't want to own up to his part of the bargain. So we thought we'd help keep him honor-able. See, a little birdie told me that ya was fetchin' a little lady for him to wed. So...I was thinkin' to myself, 'self, I wonder how

much ole Richie'll give me in exchange for his br-ide?'"
He laughed as though he smoked too many cigarettes
and nodded his greasy head towards a wide-eyed
Madeline.

David felt her trembling behind him as she grasped
firmly at his shirt. His jaw muscles flickered. No way was he
going to allow McCreedy and his boys to take her. Not
without a fight.

"Don't be an idiot McCreedy. You know Richard would
beef ya for much less." David warned as his grip tightened
on his knife wishing he'd carried his guns on him instead.

"Now, now Davey. Don't git yer back up. No sense in
gettin' yerself killt – I have no problem with you," McCreedy
said. "This is atwixt the boss and us."

The other two cocked their guns to make sure he
understood.

"Then, why bring the lady into it?" David threw at them.
Though he kept his voice low and even, Madeline could
hear the tinge of anger in his words.

McCreedy seemed stumped for a moment, then smiled
an oily smile. "Call it leve-rage, my boy. Jus' makin' certain
we get what we gots comin' to us."

Madeline's heart was beating so loud she thought they
could all hear it. *What could she do?* She couldn't let David
get hurt or die trying to protect her. The odds were three to
one. Though she knew David could wield a knife like no
one she's ever seen before, he didn't stand a chance against
three *guns*.

Reluctantly, she placed her hand on his bicep—he was
so strained. "David...don't...I'll go with them. I'll be all right...
please." she pleaded ever so softly.

David knew he could take out one, but the other two
would have him down soon after...then there would be no

hope for Madeline. If he lived now, he might be able to save her later.

"David..." she whispered. She felt the tenseness in his arm start to dissipate. He slowly looked back at her, the pain in his eyes evident. "I'm sorry...I will come for you..." he said quietly, dropped his knife, and hung his head.

Doogan swaggered over and took Madeline by the wrist, pulling her behind him none too gently, while Roy grabbed a hold of the horses.

"And just how am I s'pose to get the message to Richard without my horse?" David growled.

"Yer resourceful, Davey. You can manage...cain't have ya throttling us in the middle of the night." McCreedy explained. "You'll do well not to follow us...Oh, and I'll be takin' that there dirk of yers. Now you jus' move on back."

All David could think about was keeping Maddie safe. He backed up a few feet then said through tight lips, "If Miss Sorrells comes to any harm...ya won't have to worry about Richard...I'll kill ya myself."

McCreedy flinched a little, knowing he meant it. He cautiously walked over and snatched up the knife. Then backed his way to the horses. Once there, he smiled a tooth-less grin.

Doogan licked his lips and took Madeline's hair in his dirty fingers to smell it as he sneered at David who clenched and unclenched his fists. Madeline jerked her head away, restraining herself not to slap him, and quickly mounted Lola. Doogan let out a raspy laugh, and he kept his eye on David. Throwing his lanky leg over the saddle, he hefted himself onto his horse, and they rode away. David and Madeline's eyes locked and held each other until the party rode out of sight.

David was left alone with his few supplies, his thoughts,

and his rage. *How could he drop his guard like that?* He shook his head attempting to clear his mind. He knew McCreedy wouldn't want anything to happen to Maddie...at least not before he got his money. Roy was a follower. He would do McCreedy's bidding, but Doogan...he was a different story. There was always an evil lurking in that man's eyes. "Now what? I have no horse, no way to get to Richard...no way to save Maddie..."

"Please, Father, please protect her... and forgive me for being so careless with whatchuv entrusted to me."

12

SEARCH

David sat with his back against a tree. He stared at the ground in front of him attempting to harness his thoughts. His tracking skills were tested with the hot sun and without a horse. But, he had to keep trying. He had to get Maddie back. He tipped his canteen up to his parched lips and drank greedily. He felt the sting as sweat dripped in his eyes and coursed down his tanned face. He sloshed the water over his head and leaned back with his eyes closed.

It had been eight grueling hours since McCreedy left with her. Traveling on foot had, of course, slowed his progress tremendously. His thoughts were all over the place, like a bee in search of the perfect flower. His emotions went through phases: rage at McCreedy and the gang, anger at himself for letting them get the slip on him, fear for Madeline, and though he hated to admit it, a great sense of loss without her near.

This simply would not do! He couldn't think like a tracker with his mind in such a jumble. "That woman!" he growled. Her and her brown, doe-like eyes...her coffee-colored hair cascading down her back...her soft, pink lips smiling up at him...

Suddenly he felt a sharp object thrust into his side. "Not again..." He grudgingly stuck his hands in the air. He heard a chuckle from behind him. He pivoted around slowly to the amused face of his blood brother, Soars with Eagles. With relief in his eyes, David let out his breath and stood to his feet. "How in the world didya..."

"Your mind must be elsewhere, Hat' ê stseahe. I have not been able to sneak up on you in many moons." Soars with Eagles eyes glistened.

They grasped each other's forearms and gave a firm shake. "It is good to see you, my brother." David looked weary. "Yer right, my mind is not where it should be. I could really use yer help."

"What has happened?" his friend questioned.

"It's a long story, but believe it or not, this is the second time someone's got the jump on me today," David began. "Some of Richard's men bested me earlier. I was escortin' Mad... a young lady to Belle Rive and they bushwhacked us." He could feel the heat rising as he recalled the event. "They rode off with her, my horse, and my knife!" He slapped his stetson against his thigh. "Not to mention, my guns were stashed in the saddlebags. But somehow, I've gotta get the young lady back. I don't trust those guys to be honorable."

"How long ago?" Soars with Eagles looked intently at him.

"Since daybreak. They gotta pretty good lead." He raked his fingers through his damp hair in frustration.

Soars with Eagles turned slightly and let out a shrill whistle. Materializing from the trees, three other Cheyenne warriors made their presence known. He spoke in his native tongue to them, and one faded back into the trees. Within a minute, he came back leading two horses forward, handing one to Soars with Eagles and the other to David.

"Come, Hat' ê stseahe." He jumped onto the horse's back, motioning to David to follow suit. "I will help you find this woman."

David paused a moment in wonder at his friend. Words escaped him, and he hoped the warrior could read the relief and thanks in his eyes.

They found the trail to be easy to follow. Five sets of hoofprints clearly showed their direction to be heading south. Without his horse, they must have thought he wouldn't be an issue and didn't take care to cover their tracks.

If he knew Maddie, she would be slowing them down as much as she could. David smiled at the thought of her giving them some of the problems he had dealt with. *Too bad she wasn't wearing that cursed skirt now!*

DAVID HAD PEGGED HER RIGHT. Madeline had attempted to escape twice already. Doogan had hold of a rope tied around Lola and was riding beside her to make sure she didn't try anything. Desperately wanting to get away from her foul-mouthed, whiskey-drenched captors, and without thinking through her next step, Madeline had flung herself off of the horse and started rolling down an embankment. Though she managed to get her footing and began running towards some trees, they were on her in no time dragging her back, kicking and screaming. They plopped her on a horse with Doogan. The second attempt at escaping was when he had finished "relieving" himself and had put his foot in the stirrup to begin to hoist himself up. Madeline kicked him, causing him to stumble backward, falling onto his 'keester.' Madeline planted her heels into the horse's sides, and leaning forward to keep her balance, yelled, "Haw!" The horse took off in a gallop, which ended rather quickly with the other two in pursuit. They grabbed the reins, pulling her to an abrupt stop nearly sending her plummeting to the ground face first. She felt a hand jerk her back into a sitting position.

McCreedy's face close to hers, he hissed, "Listen lil' missy, ya try anythin' agin, and I'll bind ya so tight-like ta Doogan ya won't be able ta draw breath!" Madeline tried pulling her arm out of his grasp, but he crunched down all the tighter until she cried out. He hurled her arm away, and, as a second thought, roughly snatched the rawhide from her failing braid, causing her to yelp. He then strapped it around her wrists none too gently. "I reckon that'll keep ya put." He turned to Doogan, "Fer Pete's sake, keep a hode of er!"

"Oh, I weel," Doogan vowed as he gathered himself onto the horse. Immediately, his arm swallowed her waist in a tight grip. Grinding his whiskered cheek into hers, he slobbered into her ear, "Jist try it agin...jist try..."

Madeline was becoming sick to her stomach by the man's offensive odor. She jerked her face away from him and started thrashing about but ceased as McCreedy turned to look back at them, remembering what he threatened. She couldn't imagine being any closer to Doogan than she was at the moment, but she didn't want to take a chance. She quaked in Doogan's slimy clutch. She knew the only reason he hadn't tried anything with her because of McCreedy's fear of Richard. He had warned Doogan and Roy to be on their best behavior, or he'd "shoot em hisself!"

. . .

DAVID WAS A MAN DRIVEN. Soars with Eagles suggested they stop to water the animals, but David continued on. He couldn't shake the image of her riding off. He saw fear in her eyes and heard it in her voice as she pleaded with David to let her go. *"I'll be all right,"* she whispered to him. Could he have done more? "So help me, if they touch her...I'll kill em."

They came to a stream and David finally agreed to a short stop. They dipped their heads down into the refreshing water and took their fill of drink, then replenished the water skins Soars with Eagles had supplied. The coolness of the water gave David new vigor, and he was ready to go. Soars with Eagles insisted they eat something and rest a while first. Besides, the horses were tired. They had ridden them hard for about four hours.

"Tell me about this woman." Soars with Eagles pulled out some dried deer meat to share.

David sat back and let out a long sigh. "She's to wed Richard." He refused to call him his brother because of their history together. "I'm takin' her to him. She was put into my care, and I blew it!"

"Blew...it?" Soars with Eagles questioned not knowing the term.

"Uhhhh...failed to protect her," he explained and Soars with Eagles nodded.

"Maddie—Madeline is the most stubborn, pig-headed woman I've ever met. But at the same time, can be kind, genuine, smart, witty—and she's rather kinda pretty." David got a far off look on his face.

"Do you go to her for Richard...or for yourself, Hat' ê stseahe?" The question hung in the air for a couple of minutes.

"I go for Maddie," David replied. "I can't leave her in the custody of those outlaws. It ain't right...not in God's eyes...not in my eyes. Find her for Richard? No. He doesn't deserve her."

Soars with Eagles had a knowing look in his eyes and a smug smile pulling at his thick lips.

"Hey, now wait a minute. I know what yer thinkin'. Ya think I'm in love with her, don'tcha?" David asked, nodding. Soars with Eagles lifted his eyebrows.

"Nawww...I couldn't. She frustrates the daylights out of me. Love her..." He laughed. "Love her? I...I...nawww. It ain't possible." With that, he arose and prepared to leave.

His friend smiled and shook his head. They rode in silence following the path laid out before them. They were gaining on the group which made David push even harder.

MADELINE's three captors lazed around the fire drinking whiskey, or 'gut warmer' as they liked to call it, and telling fabricated stories to each other, but loud enough to impress their prisoner. She was far from impressed. *The poor people they tormented as they went "collecting"*...she trembled from the thought. She would have to inform Richard of what goes on. Surely he can not know. After all, he was David's brother. *Brother*...why didn't he tell her? He lied to her...or did he? He never said he wasn't. He just didn't disclose the information. She felt a spark light her eyes. He should have told her! Still, she was very thankful it was he that came collecting from her father. He had been a total gentleman, well except when he removed her skirt, but that was more her own doing. He had been right all along, but she was too stubborn to admit it. He hadn't put up with her shenanigans. He was a man she admired. *Oh, how can I marry Richard? A stranger.* From what she had been able to gather, he wasn't at all like David. He seemed very demanding.

David seemed like a bully at first, but would he have been had she not been so obstinate? Ruggedly handsome. Yes, she had noticed as soon as she allowed herself to actually look at him, and not glare through him—his curly light brown hair reaching for his shoulders, his golden-brown eyes challenging her—handsome indeed. She felt the power of his muscles when he pulled her from the river. She had felt safe in his arms...safe with him, until this. Of course, without a gun, there is nothing one can do against three. Why didn't he carry one on his person at all times? All cowboys do, don't they?

He didn't always treat her like a lady. More like a spoiled child in need of a spanking—which he had on occasion threatened to do! A flame rose in her eyes - then vanished. *David...I think I'm falling in love with you...*She drifted into a dream world where he filled her thoughts. Forgetting that she was to be another's, forgetting that she might not see him again, forgetting about her circumstances. In her dreams, he came to her rescue like the knights in shining armor she had read about as a girl. She remembered his kiss and his strong arms wrapped around her...

Booming laughter cut through her dreams and snatched her back to reality. The three men were still carrying on about their prowess and trophies. *Well, as long as they stay away from her!* she shivered. What she saw earlier in Doogan's eyes terrified her. *David, please find me.*

As the night drew on, she pretended to sleep, when in fact she was listening for when they passed out—surely it wouldn't take long with all the drinking they did. Roy was the first on watch; he was to keep an eye on her. But the whiskey got the better of him, and he soon started snoring.

Her hands still bound, she sawed at the rawhide with a sharp stone. She cut at her skin a couple of times before managing to break free. Wincing from the pain, she rubbed her wrists to get the blood circulating again. She had been thinking about which direction to go once she got loose. As they were riding, she was trying to pay attention to landmarks along the way, but, after hours of the grueling trek, it all looked the same. Knowing the east from the west and the south from the north was not her strong point. David had tried to teach her but she hadn't listened long enough to learn. *Stupid girl!* she rebuked herself. *Too prideful to admit that I don't know everything. Now look at me.* She let out a disgusted breath. "Okay...we came from that direction...well at least I know that much." It was pitch dark, so she knew it would be harder to find her way around, but she at least had to make an effort. She tried not to think about what could be lurking out there, waiting to devour her. At the moment, she was more afraid of what could devour her if she stayed.

She would have to cover a lot of ground before they awoke. She noiselessly crept up to Lola. She would have to ride bareback. She couldn't risk the time and effort to put the saddle on. "That's a good girl," she cooed. A horse snorted, she froze. *Oh, please, God - keep them asleep.* Nothing. Letting out her breath slowly, she began to lead Lola away. She couldn't manage Zeke too, so she regretfully decided to leave him behind. Every little twig that snapped amplified in her ears. Just a little further—Lola startled. Suddenly, a hand clamped over her mouth, dragging her deeper into the trees. She tried to scream. "I warned ya," a cruel voice slurred. "Now I'm gonna teach ya a lesson." Doogan flung her to the ground, which jarred her and stole her breath. Pinning her beneath him, he slobbered wet kisses all over her face as the stench of stale whiskey assailed her. His hand returned to tightly cover her mouth to prevent her from alerting the others. Terror filled her eyes, which excited him all the more.

"Oh, God! help me!" Madeline yelled inside her head. Then she managed to fasten her teeth down on one of his fingers and bit fiercely, which caused him to let up just enough so that she shrieked as loud as she could, then spit in his face. "Why you!" He hauled off and belted her on the cheek. She felt the sting and tasted the blood instantly—she thought she'd faint. In and out of consciousness, she saw as two hands yanked Doogan up, and sent him sprawling. McCreedy shoved his gun in Doogan's shocked, inebriated face. "I told ya never to touch 'er! I should make ya buzzard's food right where ya lay!" he seethed. "Now git yer *@#%! back to camp!"

McCreedy took hold of Madeline by her arms and dragged her dazed, back to camp. This time he bound her arms back around a tree and bound her feet. "She ain't goin' anywheres nohow."

Then he swaggered off to his flea trap. Pointing a crooked finger at Doogan, he warned, "Ya stay away from er'. I'll not have Richard killin' me cuz she's ruint goods."

Then she blacked out.

13

RESCUE

David and Soars with Eagles stopped abruptly—
ears straining intently. They thought they heard a
scream pierce the early morn. It was faint, some
distance from them.

"Come." Soars with Eagles had taken the lead as the
night came on as he had keener eyes to guide them.

Smoke from a fire invaded their nostrils. They were
closing in. All weariness from the hard-paced trek fell away
from them. Muscles tensed, blood began to race, adrenaline
pumped.

MADELINE COULD TASTE blood in her mouth. She wasn't sure
how long she had been out but awoke with a start to find
herself bound to a tree. Her thoughts were all hazy, but
memories came rushing back. Her arms and shoulders were
aching—her face throbbing from Doogan's hand. The sun
was starting to peek over the horizon. She looked around
the campsite; all three men were snoring away. They obviously didn't feel the need to keep watch on her now.

Clearing her wits, she remembered McCreedy, of all people, coming to her rescue. She hadn't been violated! *Thank you, God. Thank You!* A couple of tears carved a path down her swollen cheek falling to her lap. It had been almost a full day since she was taken. She had the overwhelming feeling of hopelessness start to take root in her heart. She hung her head and let the tears flow. She silently prayed, *"Oh God...what am I going to do? Please help me. Please help David somehow find me."*

DAVID AND SOARS with Eagles dismounted their horses and tethered them hastily to a tree. They would walk the rest of the way. Stealthily, they crept along the brush. Soars with Eagles was to circle to the back of the camp, while David made his way to Zeke. A horse whinnied which caused him to stiffen...still the three men slept, snoring to high heaven. He patted Zeke and spoke quietly in his ear as he eased to the horse's side. He unlatched the satchel, removed his gun belt, and strapped it on. He was to wait by the horses until Soars with Eagles was in place. A low bird call would announce when he was ready. It took everything in David to stay put. Maddie was so close—he wanted to run to her and let her know he had come for her. He wanted to riddle McCreedy, Doogan, and Roy with bullet holes from his two Colt 45's.

There it was...the signal—time to act! David emerged from the trees—guns in hand. He watched as Soars with Eagles soundlessly appeared across from him. David looked around the campsite taking note of where each man slept, then caught sight of Maddie. Her head was down, her arms tied behind her around a tree—*was she all right?* First things first—*focus man!* He shook his head to clear it. Soars with

Eagles had his bow ready. David cocked his guns. The echo sliced through the morning silence.

MADELINE LIFTED her head at the sound, searching for the object that made it. Her gaze fell on him, and she squinted, trying to make out the faint silhouette. Her heart started pounding hard against her chest. She would know that stance anywhere. "David?" she rasped. *Could it really be? Was she dreaming?* Then he spoke, and the sound was a caress wrapping around her like a warm shawl. His voice was loud and harsh, though soothing to her aching soul.

"RISE AND SHINE BOYS!" David yelled. "Hands up where I can see 'em."

"What the..." McCreedy bolted up, unsteady on his feet, his face in a scowl.

Doogan blinked several times and squinted towards David while his hand floundered around for his gun.

"I suggest ya leave the gun where it lies," David warned, then tilted his head as he grinned a bit. "Naw...on second thought, go ahead..."

McCreedy must have been a little buffaloed at David's choice of weapon; the man stood scowling at the pistol pointing at his head. David watched as McCreedy's eyes flicked to his own gun. He asked, "Jest what're ya doin' with that there gun Davey? Where's that ole trusty knife of yers? Oh... that's right. I gots it," he snickered.

"Well, McCreedy," David's voice was a low growl, "funny thing. I prefer my knife. Cleaner. But trust me. I know how to use my guns." Each of the men began to get a little antsy. David nodded towards Soars with Eagles to show himself.

"Aaack! Whatcha go an bring a dirty injun fer?" McCreedy spewed, his hate for the people evident in the disgusted look in his eyes.

Soars with Eagles kept his bow aimed at McCreedy. David knew his friend could easily take out all three men within seconds; the man's steady and stoic gaze letting them know just that. Keeping one gun in hand, David collected all the weapons. Then holstering his second gun, he hurried to Maddie's side. Her tear-stained, weary face looked up at him with such relief it nearly undid him. He quickly untied the ropes that bound her hands and feet. Then gently helped her to stand. She rubbed at her arms and shoulders, trying to soothe the strained muscles. He took hold of her chin, examining the nasty bruise on her right side of her face. His jaw clenched. "Who did this?"

"Doogan..." was all she got out when David shot across the camp. Taking Doogan off guard, David caught him on the jaw, knocking him to the ground. Then he kicked him hard in the ribs on both sides. He dropped to the ground over Doogan and began punching him again and again, certainly breaking his nose. Doogan was crying out for help. But the only one who took pity on him was the one he had aimed to hurt.

Madeline rushed over and pulled on David's shirt. "David, please! That's enough, David!" He stopped mid-punch as she broke through to him.

He slowly raised himself up. "Don't you ever come near her again...or I'll kill ya," he said between clenched teeth.

Doogan lay there, a whimpering, crumbled lump. McCreedy and Roy looked on with mouths agape. "Didn't know ya had it in ya, boy," McCreedy said.

David fired a warning glare at him. His muscles were still pumped and tense, and anything could set him off. He walked with purpose over to McCreedy's satchel and retrieved his knife as Soars with Eagles searched for hidden weapons. Then David grabbed a blanket, wrapped it around Madeline, and held her tightly as she cried—the anxiety and fear of the last twenty-four hours gushing deep from within her. David lightly kissed her forehead and smoothed her matted hair. "Shh...it's alright. It's over now." He swallowed a lump in his own throat. It truly was over.

"Well ain't that a purdy picture. Yer brother won't take kindly to ya holdin' his lady like that." McCreedy spit.

David wordlessly hefted his gun as he pivoted himself and Maddie around. He was pointing it directly at McCreedy's forehead—tempted. "No," lowering and holstering his gun again, "I'll leave ya to Richard. Yer as good as dead already."

Then he helped Madeline mount up on Zeke. She was too unsteady and shaken to ride alone, and he wasn't ready to let her. He swung himself up behind her. Gently engulfing her in his arms, he took hold of the reins. Soars with Eagles latched Lola to Zeke's saddle, then shooed McCreedy's horses off. No weapons. No horses. Nice turn of events. David smiled at the thought.

"Hey, now Davey," McCreedy said, realizing the predicament he was in, "No need in spillin' to Richard. Ya got whatcha came fer."

David shot him a deadly look which was anything but reassuring. Then turned the horses to leave as McCreedy and Roy attended to a broken and bloody Doogan.

Relief flooded over David, and he began to unwind. Maddie settled into his arms resting the back of her head against his chest. She was safe. *Thank You, God.*

14

CONFESSION

Madeline was exhausted. She had fallen asleep in David's arms, wrapped in a cocoon of security. She hadn't even noticed when David and Soars with Eagles parted company. She had hoped to thank the stoic Indian—the tall, lean man with the piercing dark eyes. She had never seen one in the wild but had always heard tales about their cruelty to settlers and savage ways. At first, he had unsettled her, but she remembered David's stories of his Cheyenne friends. If David trusted him, then she would. The man, after all, aided in her rescue.

After a few hours, she struggled to open her eyes. She startled, realizing she was back on a horse with a man's arms around her. Her eyes darted about, and her heart quickened. Had she dreamt of the rescue? Panic seized her until she heard, "Shhh...it's alright, Maddie. Yer safe." She heard the name 'Maddie' and knew she was with David; his soft voice soothed her. She was safe. David had come for her, and God had protected her. She shuddered involuntarily. David brought the horses to a stop.

"Here. Let's rest for a while." He slid off behind her.

Then taking hold of her waist, gently lifted her down. He did not release her, for which she was glad. She felt unsteady. Her legs were shaking; her whole body hurt! She searched his eyes, then threw herself into his arms. She needed his strength. He enveloped her in a tight embrace, wedging out all of the terrifying memories.

David had wrestled with his thoughts all morning as she slept. *Did he love her?* Though he had told himself he couldn't, he couldn't deny it now—with her in his arms. He could feel her trembling. He gently kissed the top of her head as his hands glided across her back. "Maddie, yer alright...I'm here." He kissed her forehead, then with one hand, cupped her tear-streaked face, and kissed her black and blue cheek, wincing at the picture it brought to his mind. Then his lips sought her quivering lips—tenderly at first, then more fervently as she responded to him. Ever so slightly, he pulled away to look into her big, brown eyes. "Maddie...I..." he paused, "somewhere along the way...I fell in love with you."

Her eyes widened under his intense gaze. Then she whispered, "And I love you..." She lifted her lips to meet his again.

Losing himself in her kisses, he tried to disregard the still, small voice speaking to his heart. *She does not belong to you.* Finally, unable to ignore the prodding any longer, he reluctantly let loose of her and backed away.

Sighing, he began unsteadily, "Maddie...this is wrong. No matter how much I desire it...it's wrong."

She was breathless and weak-kneed, this time from being immersed in a lover's embrace. "But I love *you*, David."

"You belong to Richard. You are to marry him." He tried to convince himself as much as her.

"I belong to *no* man yet! I don't even know Richard." She dropped to the ground in a heap, her head hung low, and her shoulder's cowed.

"Maddie..." David bent down on a knee, but not too close, fearing what her nearness might do to his already weak senses. "I'm sorry. Yer right. You don't belong to anybody. But think. There is a written contract between Richard and yer father. Richard will hold to it. So, yer as good as his."

She waved a hand as to dismiss the fact, then nailing him with a hard stare, asked, "Speaking of Richard, how come you didn't mention that he was your brother?"

He stiffened, a look of chagrin on his face, "I'm sorry I didn't tell ya. I thought it would cause you more pain."

A sliver of hope passed through his mind. He would ask Richard to accept his services for two more years, and then he could marry Maddie himself! Could it work? Would Richard take the agreement? Could he stand to work for Richard two more years? Yes. He could. If it meant he could have the woman he loved by his side. He couldn't mention this to Maddie until he talked to Richard. He couldn't get her hopes up...or his.

"We will hope and pray for things to work out differently for us. But, in the meantime," David grinned, "we've gotta keep our distance." He rose and lent a hand to help her to her feet, then turned to busy himself elsewhere.

She lowered her head and smiled. He was right. The two of them alone together for at least three more days—anything could happen if they weren't careful. They could not allow things to get out of control. They would have to harness their feelings.

Though David didn't want to stay put long, he did build a fire and warmed some water for bouillon. He still had some dried meat left that they could share. Later, when they stopped for the night, he would snare a rabbit to make some stew. For now, this would have to do.

Maddie had curled up by the fire and fallen back to sleep. She looked very small and vulnerable now. He would respect her. He had no right kissing her like that. He found himself wishing for his friend, Soars with Eagles to appear and protect him from himself.

While the water simmered he propped himself against a rock and watched as Maddie slept. He was beyond tired, but still wasn't ready to take his eyes off her.

AFTER GETTING BACK into the routine of riding, Madeline pulled Lola up to walk beside Zeke and said, "Tell me about Richard...your brother." She quirked an eyebrow. "He seems so cruel... and I'm to be his wife. Does he know God at all?"

David couldn't lie to Maddie. "No. He doesn't want anything to do with Him. Our parents didn't raise us in the church, and, when they died, money became Richard's god." David frowned, "He's not...a nice man, Maddie. He won't appreciate yer 'stubborn streak' as I do." He tossed her a smile to make light of it. But, it quickly fell from his lips as he looked her in the eyes and said, "Please ask God to help you respect him."

Madeline wanted to protest but knew she couldn't. God had been trying to deal with her on her temper and independent spirit. It was a problem. She quivered involuntarily. "I will pray, David, and I will try."

Now it was David's turn to falter. "Ya know, Maddie..." he pondered for a moment. "I would like nothing better than to turn around and take ya away...far from Richard." He got quiet for a moment. "Say the word," he looked her dead in the eyes, "and I'll do it."

Oh, how she would love to say "yes." Her heart jumped at the chance, but her mind knew she couldn't. Her father...yes, her father, as awful as he may seem, needed her to go through with this arrangement. His life depended on her doing it. She couldn't live with the thought of him dead when she could have saved him. She loved him still. She tried to push him out of her thoughts, but he kept forcing his way in. If she could just forget him, it would be so easy to run off with David and become *his* wife. She liked the thought of that...but she couldn't allow herself to dwell on it. Because then, they'd be on the run for the rest of their days. Not only her father's life would be in jeopardy but David's as well. No. She couldn't do it.

"I know, David. And I thank you. But we both know I can't let you do that."

His eyes searched hers.

"My father," she addressed the question she read in his eyes, "and...because you would become a hunted man."

"I can outsmart Richard and his goons. I'll be alright. Let me protect you." He knew it was a losing argument. She was right, but he had to try. She had bucked him many times, but always gave way when he pointed out the truth. He had grown to admire her and all her stubborn ways. She yielded when it was important. Would she do the same for Richard? He feared for her. Richard would demand respect, not earn it.

Madeline was thinking along the same lines. Here before her sat a strong man, firm, but gentle and with godly character. He was everything she desired in a husband. He earned her respect, which did not come easy. At this moment, she was weak, and he was too near...his eyes begging her to say yes. *No! She couldn't.*

"David. Please don't. I'm not as strong as you think," she touched his arm. "Don't you know I would like nothing better than to run? To be with you? But I can't." Her head bent down. "Please help me to be strong."

Her stomach had been feeling uneasy all day. They were less than a day and a half away from Belle Rive. Her new life terrified her. *Oh, God.* She silently pleaded with the heavens. *Please change Richard's mind; let him not want me. I want to be with David!* How could she live without him? How could she be another man's wife? *God, please let me have this. Everything else has been taken from me. David loves me, and I love him.* She held onto the slightest hope. If God really cared for her, He'd do this, wouldn't He? Her confidence faltered. She had prayed a similar prayer for her mother and brother...and they died. She had prayed for her father to love her and to not gamble anymore...now look where his gambling got her. She had begged and pleaded with God not to make her take this journey, yet here she was.

Hot tears began to pool in her eyes. It was useless to fight them. They were tears of anger from all the hurt and disappointments. She then determined that if God didn't help her in this—she didn't want anything to do with Him ever again.

David was also praying; his prayers were vastly different from Maddie's. *God. You know my heart. You know my desires. But no matter what happens, I will trust in You.*

15

RICHARD

Richard paced the floor impatiently. David should have been here over a week ago with his new bride. Plus, McCreedy, Doogan, and Roy were overdue. *What was going on?* He stopped in front of the door as if willing them to come. His little brother was pushing it. If he didn't show up soon, Richard would add more time to his contract...somehow. He was given one month to get the young lady here. Not that Richard lacked female companionship; he had a woman anytime he wished it, which was often. He wasn't planning on that stopping just because he had a wife. He needed sons, and she would provide them for him.

"Rich-ard...come back to bed," a rich, sultry voice called.

He walked into the room where the sensual Sylvia was lying across rumpled covers. He picked up her clothes and threw them at her. "Get dressed." He turned to leave. "Then, get out."

Sylvia looked hurt. He was in a foul mood now, but later...he'd want her back. Maybe she'd just say no—tell him to go elsewhere! But no one said no to Richard. She knew that well. She quickly dressed and tried to make herself presentable before slipping out the back door.

MADDIE WAS STALLING FOR TIME, and David knew it. They had stopped three times in the last hour. Once to clean herself up before arriving at her new home and twice to "relieve" herself. Now, she was asking again, insisting that they must stop so she could straighten out her undergarments and put on her last remaining skirt before meeting Richard. She did have a point. Richard would not like that David had her wearing britches, no matter how practical it was.

"All right, " he sighed. "But this is the last time." He was being torn in two. He wanted desperately to run away with Maddie and save her from her fate with Richard. But, he knew his brother. He wouldn't stop until David was dead. No one double-crossed him. If it were just his life in danger, he'd do it in a minute. But, Madeline's low-down, rotten father would die also, and no telling what Richard would do to her once he found them. She was legally his. David's only hope was to take her to him and offer himself to Richard in service for her hand. What would Richard do? David had a sinking feeling. He had not heard from God on the matter and dreaded what that meant.

MADELINE AND DAVID hadn't spoken of their love since they first confessed it. He longed to take her in his arms and tell her everything was going to be all right. But, he didn't know that for sure. He didn't know what the future held; only God did.

When Madeline appeared, David whistled. "Ya sure look pretty, Maddie." She wanted to wear her yellow dress for David but knew that it wasn't very sensible while riding a horse.

She blushed. "Thank you." Then she took her time getting back in the saddle. David said nothing. He understood.

As they drew closer, David could see Belle Rive on the horizon. From this location, it looked so peaceful nestled up to a mountain. But, he knew it was anything but peaceful. He pointed it out to Maddie, who mumbled, "It's beautiful."

Madeline felt like she was going to be sick. She hadn't eaten all day, and that, mixed with the anxiety she felt, had her stomach in an uproar. She felt the noose tightening around her neck. For an instant, she wanted to take David up on his earlier offer and forget about everything...about Richard, her father, the contract... but...she couldn't. She willed herself on and clicked her heels under Lola—a determined look overtaking her features, a callousness settling in her heart. She refused to meet David's gaze.

David noticed the change in her, but didn't know whether to applaud her effort, or tremble at her resignation.

RICHARD SAW them in the distance and started barking orders to his ranch hands and housemaid, Mabel. "Good for you, little brother," he smirked. He stood on the massive, stone porch with his arms folded across his chest, legs spread apart. He had a cigar clenched in his teeth.

When they were directly in front of him, David dismounted with barely a look in Richard's direction and went around to help Madeline down.

"I can manage. Thank you, Mr. Shelton." She showed

him half a smile, and gracefully threw her leg around behind her and stepped down.

David noticed the formality and how she stood rigidly with a strained look on her face.

He moved toward Richard. "Richard." They grasped hands with a firm shake. "David." Richard returned.

"This is Mad...Miss Sorrells," David introduced them.

"Miss Sorrells. It is a pleasure to finally meet you." He reached out for her hand and kissed the back of it. He looked her over which made Madeline cringe inside.

She wasn't as pretty as he had hoped. Shame. But, though on the thin side, she did have a fine figure with all the right curves. He winked at her, and she withdrew her hand. "Is there somewhere I might freshen up? I fear I must look dreadful after such a tiring journey." Really, she just wanted an excuse to get away from him.

"Mabel!" he hollered. "Please show Miss Sorrell's to her room," he said as the plump, kind-faced housekeeper appeared, "I need to talk to my little brother." David hated the way he always said "little brother."

"Yes, sir. This way Miss Sorrells." The first thing Madeline had noticed about Richard was his immaculate attire. He was in dark, pinstriped pants with a white shirt and dark vest over it. He had a red necktie pushed snugly up to his chin. His dark brown hair was neatly trimmed and combed with hair grease, unlike David's unkempt curls. He had a well-groomed mustache, and dark, ill-tempered eyes. They made her shiver under their gaze. He was a couple of inches taller than David and built slightly larger. He was rather handsome, but his gaze unsettled her. His lips on her hand felt...*oh what's the word*...cold...not warm and tender like David's touch. Maybe, she was just adding feeling to what she had heard of Richard...maybe, he really wasn't that bad...

The house was lavishly decorated. Rich colors, dark reds, browns, and golds. Mahogany wood furniture all around. Grander than she could have ever imagined. Even with all the warm colors...the place felt steely, unwelcoming to her. Thoughts of where all these furnishings came from assaulted her mind and sent her reeling.

Mabel showed her to a large, master suite, rather masculine looking, with a four-poster bed in the center. "This'll be your room with Mr. Shelton."

Madeline abruptly stopped. "You mean *after* we're wed."

"Ahhh...," Mabel looked confused.

"I'll talk to Mr. Shelton about it, Mabel," Madeline assured her. "Please show me the rest of the house."

Upstairs, Mabel took her to a good-sized room with lace curtains, decorated in a soft yellow and pale blue. "This was Mrs. Shelton's favorite room—Richard and David's mother."

"I can see why." It felt peaceful there. Safe. She would ask Richard if this could be her special room.

"I WAS EXPECTING you over a week ago," Richard said sternly. "I was beginning to think your morals kept you from doing what you were told to do."

"I'm not happy about transporting human cargo to ya. And yer right, I almost didn't go through with it."

"But in the long run, your freedom was more important, ain't that right?" He struck up a match to relight his cigar.

"No, Richard. It was the fact that another man's life was on the line, and Miss Sorrells insisted she go through with it," David made clear.

"Good girl," Richard sneered, nodding his head. "Of

course, you know what would have happened if you took what belongs to me."

"It wasn't me I was concerned about," David said. "I would, however, like to talk about my freedom now."

"Later." Richard blew smoke out. "Why were you late?"

"Well, Richard," David stretched out under a tree. "Seems you got McCreedy, Doogan, and Roy a little upset. Somethin' about 30 silver pieces..."

A sharp glare took over Richard's countenance.

"They decided that until ya pay them what was due, they would take yer bride hostage." He stuck a blade of grass in his mouth as he waited for Richard's response.

"Just what do you mean, 'take her'?" he demanded.

"They caught me off guard," David threw the grass to the ground, "and took Madeline at gunpoint." He was careful not to use Maddie. He didn't want Richard thinking they got too personal. "They took my horse and my knife figurin' I'd find a way to get to ya with their demands. Instead, I went after them."

Richard's chest was heaving in and out. The muscles in his jaws were flickering.

"She was a little worse for wear when I found 'em, but seemed all right. Doogan had belted her one for reasons I didn't ask. But, I did make him pay." He knew he had just sealed Doogan's fate, as well as the others. *Forgive me, God.*

"So, you killed him."

"No. I didn't. But I left him pretty banged up. There is never a good reason to hit a woman." David made that point rather sternly.

"I want them dead," Richard said without blinking an eye. Then, he exploded and began airin' his lungs, "How dare they steal from me, and make demands of me!"

His anger had nothing to do with Maddie. It was all about what they did to him. That infuriated David.

"You should have killed them. Now you'll just have..."

He didn't get a chance to finish. David had cut him off as he stood to brush off his backside. "I'm done, Richard. This was my last job for ya...unless..."

"Unless what?" Richard's eyebrows went up.

Okay God...here we go...

"I'll work for ya...for two more years if...ya let Madeline's father out of the contract, and let her choose who she would like to marry."

Richard threw back his head and guffawed loudly. "Meaning *you*, right?" Then, in a dead-serious tone said, "No. I need a wife to bear my sons. I own her, and she will do my bidding. I'll find someone else to take care of McCreedy."

He started to walk off when David caught him by his arm. "Richard, please don't make her go through with this."

"You have my answer. I appreciate you taking care of my investment, but your job here is done." Richard looked down at the hand grasping him and raised daring eyes at his brother.

David dropped his arm. He knew to go further would only anger Richard and could make things worse for everyone involved.

"Oh, and little brother..." Richard stopped and faced him, taking his cigar out of his mouth. "If she ain't as pure as the driven snow...I'll kill you...and her." He popped the cigar back in his mouth and strolled away.

16

DISAPPOINTMENT

M adeline sought solace over the past week in the one room she felt secure. She slept in it until she was expected to join Richard. The room was bright and pleasant—more feminine than the rest of the house. She often woke to the cheery sight of a vase full of fresh-cut flowers—Mabel's doing. The woman had already become very dear to her. She always had a shoulder to cry on, chubby, loving arms to embrace her and kind words to soothe her. She reminded Madeline of her mother. Oh, how she wished her mother were here now!

Richard kept his distance, which she appreciated. At least he honored that wish. They honestly hadn't spent much time together since she had arrived. He didn't seem interested in really getting to know her as a person. He did let her know, in no uncertain terms, that her father's life *and* David's was in her hands—if she didn't go through with the wedding or tried anything. Oh! She couldn't believe his cruelty. How could he and David have come from the same loins? It was inconceivable to her.

MADELINE HAD HOPED and prayed for a miracle, yet here she was...standing beside Richard. The grim-faced parson just pronounced them man and wife. It didn't seem real. It had to be a nightmare that she'd wake up from any moment. No. The kiss was real enough. Cold, like Richard.

Right at that moment, she hardened her heart. Never again would she ask God for help. She didn't want anything to do with Him. All she wanted was David. She had begged God to let her marry him, and now...now she was *Richard's* wife. God had failed her for the last time.

Madeline felt numb. She saw a tear slide down Mabel's cheek as the woman hung her head. Dear, sweet Mabel. She had tried to prepare Madeline the best she could to become Richard's wife when it had seemed inevitable. Over and over, she had begged Madeline to respect him and watch the way she responded. In other words, "hold your tongue." It would be a difficult task since she hated him.

The celebration went on for hours after the ceremony. Richard was busy entertaining their guests. All were drinking, especially him. Madeline had excused herself early and took refuge in her room. She sat dazed in front of the vanity looking into hollow eyes for a long time. Then, in a detached stupor, she unleashed her hair from its pins, letting it spill over her white shoulders down her back. She changed into a revealing, red, satin gown that Richard had given to her. She felt exposed.

She heard Richard saying goodbye to the last of their guests and then stumble through the house.

"Where's my wife?" He slurred as he yelled up the stairs.

She flinched at the sound. She took a deep breath, stood, and put on a matching covering. "Please just let him pass out," she said under her breath. She went to the door, and slowly, methodically, descended the stairs.

Richard was swaying back and forth at the bottom. "There you are," he said. "Red becomes you, my darling." He reached for her hand and slobbered all over the back of it. "Your bed...is now with me." He pulled her towards their suite.

Her heart pounded so loud it hurt her ears. *Please just pass out,* she silently wished again.

LONG AFTER RICHARD had fallen into a deep slumber, Madeline lay wide awake, quietly weeping. She was Richard's wife in name and body, but not in heart. She had never felt more alone and unloved. *Oh, David...* This wasn't the way she imagined it to be. All of her dreams since she was a little girl were shattered in a matter of hours. She never knew what to expect her first time with a man since her mother had died early. She never had *that* talk. She thought from reading the Song of Solomon that it was supposed to be beautiful, pleasurable...but she felt cheap and used. She trembled at remembering...she suddenly felt nauseated...she fought to will her stomach into submission.

Richard grunted and turned to face her...his mouth hanging open as he slept. The smell of stale liquor on his breath caused Madeline's hand to fly to her mouth as she sprang from the sheets. She barely made it into the hallway before falling to her knees with dry heaves. She hadn't been able to eat or drink hardly anything the last twenty-four hours in dread of this day becoming a reality. The dry heaves racked her body until every muscle in her stomach ached. She feared she'd awaken Richard, but heard him snoring away, dead to the world. She settled back against the wall drawing her legs to her. She hung her head and sobbed violently.

The nights that followed, Richard demanded of her. His hunger was never satisfied. She didn't experience any tenderness or affection from him. She had hoped that over time she could maybe grow to love him, and he love her in return, but each passing day, even that shred of hope faded...

EARLY ONE MORNING, a couple of men Madeline didn't recognize came with a wagon weighed down full of Richard's "earnings." Madeline had never seen a load come in before and didn't care to see one now. She heard Richard barking orders. She turned from the window and headed downstairs to the kitchen to see if she could assist Mabel and distract herself.

"Good morning, Mabel," she inhaled deeply, "something sure smells delightful."

"Mornin' sugar," Mabel smiled as she pulled a tray out of the oven. "That yer smellin' is my famous honey buns."

"Mmmmm...well if they taste as good as they smell my girlish figure may soon go to the wayside." Her mouth began to water as her stomach let out a low growl.

"You could do with a few pounds on ya." Mabel shot a concerned look towards Madeline, "You're nothin' but skin and bones. I was sure hopin' my honey buns would do the trick. You've hardly eaten a thing since the wedding."

"I know, I know." Madeline sighed as she reached for a bun. "May I?"

"Of course, dear. Help yourself."

"Until this morning, even the thought of food has made me sick to my stomach." She pulled a small bite from the warm morsel. Then, practically gulped down the rest, surprised at how hungry she was.

Mabel chuckled and continued frying up some sausage and bacon. "I didn't want to interfere, but ya sure had me worried...cooped up in yer room all day and eaten nothin'."

Madeline licked the sweet, sticky goo off her fingers. "That was amazing!" Washing quickly, she began to crack some eggs in a bowl.

Richard and the guys came in and scarfed down their breakfast then got back to work, leaving Madeline and Mabel to clean up.

AFTER A WHILE, all the commotion in the large room piqued Madeline's curiosity. She peered around the door and saw several men hauling a beautiful piano in towards a corner that had recently held a writing desk. The sight sent icy shivers down her spine knowing that instrument was ripped away from a family. Though she had always wanted to learn piano, she vowed never to touch the thing.

Hurriedly, she made her way up the stairs to her sanctuary, closing the door securely behind herself. Seeing firsthand things brought into her new home from Richard's dealings caused the honey buns to sit heavily in her belly. Her eyes automatically were drawn to the window—she glimpsed a baby carriage...porcelain dolls, a beautifully crafted grandfather clock, settee, armoire, tables...

She startled as she heard heavy footsteps ascending the stairs. Richard burst in, something shiny dangling from his fingers. "There you are, my dear," strolling over to her, he held up a delicate gold chain with an emerald encased in gold filigree swinging from it. "Something beautiful to bring out your eyes."

Madeline stared in horror...*he honestly expected her to wear this?* "I...I don't want it." She turned back towards the window, then yelped as he grabbed her arm and spun her around to face him. Something hard came over his already cold eyes. "Do not refuse a gift, wife. Now lift your hair." With shaky hands, Madeline obeyed. His gaze bore into her. After clasping it on her neck, his fingers tightened on her skin as he pulled her into a lingering, passionless kiss. His kiss became more demanding until she relented and responded to him, which is what he wanted. It was becoming a game with Richard. He would push his advances on her until she gave in. Abruptly, he pushed away. "There now. It looks lovely on you. We are entertaining tonight. Make sure you dress for the occasion." With that, he smirked and left a trembling Madeline in his wake. He hadn't actually hurt her before, but she believed it was only a matter of time.

All through the evening, Madeline felt the necklace weighing heavily upon her. She found it hard to focus on any conversation—not that they tried to include her anyway. After a while, she believed she was only there because Richard wanted to exercise control over her. Finally, she couldn't stand it any longer and excused herself and made haste up the stairs. She barely made it into her room before she clawed at the piece of jewelry and yanked it from her neck. She flung the offending piece across the room. At last, she was able to breathe!

She thought about everything in the house. Other than this solace, where David's mother lovingly chose each object, each decoration—the memories of those who lost everything assaulted her. How was she to live in such a place...tormented every time she turned around. It felt like a rock took up residence in her stomach. How was she going to survive?

MADELINE RARELY SAW DAVID. She knew he was still around —she heard his name mentioned by the ranch hands and caught glimpses of him from time to time. It helped knowing he was close by. She had been afraid he would leave her as soon as they arrived at Belle Rive. She longed to talk to him, but what could she say? She was Richard's wife. David had no place in her life anymore. That thought felt like a knife to her already wounded heart.

So, Madeline spent a lot of her time with Mabel either cooking or working in the garden. It was what she most looked forward to each day—a break from her mundane existence. Of course, Mabel always tried to bring God into the picture, but Madeline would flash her a look that said, "I'm not interested. Don't even bother." Mabel would huff and say something long and drawn out under her breath like, "I don't know why she wants to shut God out at a time like this when she needs Him the most, I really don't...doesn't make a lick of sense to me whatsoever..."

Madeline couldn't help but giggle at the chubby, lovable woman. After all, she only wanted what was best for her, and Madeline knew it.

One day, she talked Mabel into joining her for a horseback ride. Madeline had an older, gentler mare named Sonja saddled up for Mabel, and she, like always, rode Lola. You would have thought Mabel had never been horseback riding before (it had been over twenty years ago!) the way she carried on. It took two ranch hands to help her mount up, and then they had to show her how to hold the reins to control the horse. Thank goodness Sonja was so easy going, or Mabel would have ended up on her hind end! She truly was a sight to behold— waddling side to side, flopping back and forth. By the end of the ride, she finally started to look more at ease, but Madeline had never heard so much complaining before in her life.

Mabel grumbled about her bottom being sore for a week. Every time she went to sit down, she had a pillow with her. Madeline joked about them riding together again from time to time but knew Mabel would never take her up on it. She'd leave all the "gallivanting around for the younger folk."

17

BEATING

Madeline came back from town one day and found their bedroom door closed during the middle of the afternoon. Thinking it odd, she opened it and found Richard sitting on the edge of their bed buttoning his shirt, with some woman perched beside him wrapped in the covers. Madeline's pulse quickened. Heat spread from her toes to her cheeks like a geyser ready to blow. Before she could stop herself, she yelled, "How dare you!" The fire in her eyes returned after a long absence. "This is OUR bed! I am your wife! Get her out of here!"

Richard turned to Sylvia, "Get dressed. I will see you later." Then turned livid eyes on Madeline. Pulling himself suddenly from the bed, he stormed toward her. He yanked her by the arm and dragged her to another room. Shutting the door, he turned around and slapped her so hard she stumbled backward. Her hand flew to her face. Her fingers immediately touched the sticky, red substance.

He towered over her, seething. "Don't you ever raise your voice to me again. I am the man of this house. I will do as I please. Do you understand me?" he said through gritted teeth.

"Ye...yes, Richard," she stammered, still in shock.

He stomped from the room, eyes still ablaze.

Madeline stumbled to shaky feet and fled from the house. She didn't know where she was running to, but she ran and ran hard, much like the night she found out what her father had done. Ranch hands were looking at her, but she didn't care. Hot tears burned down her cheeks.

DAVID COULDN'T FATHOM why he stayed. It had been weeks since he first arrived with Maddie...Richard's wife. It was a torment he couldn't break away from. He kept his distance but watched her from afar. He felt protective of her. He needed to make sure she was going to be all right.

He had just turned his head in the direction of the house when he saw Maddie running from it with her hand to her face. Richard was nowhere in sight. He hurried to the stable and saddled his horse, then tore off after her. David spotted her up ahead, lying in a heap under a tree. As he neared he heard her sobbing, her shoulders convulsing and shaking. His heart breaking, he dismounted and ran to her. "Maddie..what happened? Are ya alright?"

She was startled to hear a masculine voice behind her. She turned red, watery eyes on him, and after realizing it was David, threw herself into his arms, crying harder. "Oh, David...take me away from here," she petitioned him. "Please, please...let's go now."

As he cradled her, he asked, "What happened?" One look at her cheek and he knew. His eyes narrowed, his blood pumping faster. He pulled her to her feet and turned towards Zeke. "I'll kill 'im."

She grabbed hold of his arm. "No! Please, David. Let's just go!"

David stood, clenching and unclenching his fists, fiery eyes fixed on tear-filled ones. He reluctantly yielded, stamping down the bile that rose in his throat. Grabbing her gently by her tiny waist, he lifted her onto Zeke, then hoisted himself up behind her. Taking hold of the reins, he turned them away from Belle Rive. He rode fiercely with Maddie anchored against his chest. Only when they were miles away from the ranch did he let up.

As her mind began to clear, Madeline realized what she had done. She put David's life in jeopardy, not to mention her own. She sat upright. "Stop."

Tensing, he slowed Zeke and brought him to a halt. "What's wrong?" He dropped down, then assisted her out of the saddle.

Not wanting to look in his eyes, afraid she'd lose her resolve if she did, she said, "We have to go back."

"No." He took hold of her chin and lifted her face to his. She still wouldn't look at him. "I won't let him hurt ya again."

"You don't understand." She broke free from his hold and turned away. He dropped his hands to his side. "I am his wife, no matter how much I wish it to be different." She paused. "He told me he'd kill you if I tried anything." She turned back to him. "I've put you in danger. We must go back."

"I don't care, Maddie." He took a step toward her.

"But, I do!" she shouted, then softened, "I could not live with myself if something happened to you." She wiped vigorously at the tears spilling down her face. "I didn't respect him as you and Mabel had warned. I made a mistake. I know what to do differently now." She was pacing back and forth as David watched her. "It just took me by surprise to find another woman in our bed."

"Sylvia," David said knowingly.

Madeline looked as though he'd slapped her.

"I had hoped all that would come to an end after he married...I am sorry." David pictured the blond, chesty woman from the town saloon. "She's been around a while."

She was exasperated. "Why didn't he marry her then?"

"Ya don't marry girls like Sylvia. They ain't the marryin' kind," he confessed.

Shaking her head sadly, she said, "Nevertheless, I have to go back. I now know what to expect...and what is expected of me."

"Do you know what you're askin' of me?" His eyebrows creased in disbelief.

"I'm sorry I got you involved, David. I wasn't thinking straight. Now I am." She gently touched his face. "Please take me to the house." It certainly wasn't a 'home.'

Every moment that passed, she worried that Richard would show up and kill David right before her eyes. "Please." She pulled herself shakily up onto Zeke.

After a moment or two of brooding, David ran his hand through his hair in exasperation. Resigned, he stiffly climbed upon Zeke, turning him in the direction of Belle Rive. In silence, they began the dreaded trek back.

RICHARD'S icy stare and tense stance met them as they rode up. Stomping over, he grabbed Madeline's arm and yanked her from the horse. David put his hand to his gun and started to climb down, when Richard, with his free hand, thrust his already cocked gun up into David's face.

"Please don't, Richard," Madeline entreated. "Please. I'll do anything! It wasn't his fault. I ran. He followed me and brought me back," she spoke rapidly trying to get it all out.

"Liar," he spit at her while twisting her arm.

"Richard, stop. She tells the truth. Nothing happened."

Richard's eyes bulged, and his face reddened. "I don't believe either of you." His hand was shaking from rage. David knew Richard was in a fight with himself, not to pull the trigger. "She's my wife. And I don't want you anywhere near her! Now leave this property before I kill ya!"

"All right, Richard." His breath was coming out in short bursts—more from anger than fear. "I'll leave...just don't hurt her. She was hurt and confused when I found h...."

"I said git!"

David eased back in the saddle and led Zeke away. He feared for Maddie more than ever now. Richard was behaving irrationally. He should have ignored her pleas to take her back and kept going. His knuckles were white from his grip on the reins.

Richard had motioned to a few men standing around. They immediately took off in the same direction as David. Jeremiah, the ranch overseer, had seen the exchange. So did Madeline, but it was too late. David was out of sight, and Richard was hauling her inside. She caught a glimpse of a concerned Mabel and tried to smile to reassure her.

In their bedroom, Richard unleashed his fury on her. There was nothing she could do to shield herself. She was at his mercy. She hoped David got away...

RICHARD SENT an anxious Mabel in to attend his wife, "And don't you go coddling her. She got what she deserved."

Mabel rushed to Madeline's side. Gently helping her to stand, she led her to the bed. She was unsteady and shaking like a leaf. Her nose and mouth were bleeding, and bruises began to show up all over her body. Mabel poked around on her ribs. "Nothin' seems broken, thank God, but bruised ribs are pretty painful too."

Madeline winced as she continued examining her. "Oh, dear child," she cooed as she wrapped her chubby arms around the weeping girl. "What has he done..."

DAVID SUSPECTED Richard would do something, so he wasn't totally caught off guard when three of his henchmen surrounded him. He got in some good punches, but in the end was out numbered and succumbed to the vicious beating. They didn't kill him, but brought him to the point of wishing they had. Still, his thoughts went to Maddie. "Please God..." he faded out.

JEREMIAH RUSHED to the broken and bleeding David shortly after the beating. He had been the overseer of the ranch since David was a young boy. He was gruff, but kindhearted, and he always had a soft spot for David. He managed to get him back to his shabby cabin and sprang into action, caring for his wounds. David's nose was obviously broken. His eyes were swollen shut. He had three broken ribs and many nasty bumps and bruises. He was unconscious, which helped Jeremiah to be able to tend to the worst of his injuries. He was laid up for two weeks. No one ever knew he was there, except Madeline. David had asked about her, but Jeremiah wouldn't give him any news, only that she never wanted to see him again. Richard's doing...

As soon as David felt well enough to ride, he saddled up and left for the Dakota's. He couldn't risk staying around and letting Richard find him. Plus, he couldn't stand around knowing that Madeline was being mistreated. He felt like less of a man because he wasn't able to protect her. *She's not yours to protect,* a voice spoke to his heart. That got his attention. The statement was true. But he couldn't help wishing she was...

18

MEMORIES

Madeline received news of David's departure and took to her room. She knew about the beating. She heard the men tell Richard "it was done," and that, "he lived, as far as they knew." When they went back later to make sure, he was already gone. She knew he was held up at old Jeremiah's cabin but never risked going to see him. She got daily reports from Jeremiah on his progress and was relieved he would be alright.

But now, Jeremiah told her David had left for good—left her. Sure, she had sent word that she never wanted to see him again. But, that was for his protection. Still, she had hoped he would stay. It helped to know he was near; it made her feel more secure. But, he had deserted her...just like God. *That's not fair to say!* Her heart screamed, but her mind refused to listen.

MADELINE TRULY DID LEARN A LESSON. She kept her mouth

shut as Sylvia and other women shared Richard's bed. She learned to be content up in her room. At night, however, she was expected to be at Richard's side. She loathed him almost as much as she feared him. But, she did her wifely duties while disconnecting herself from her emotions.

There was one other mistake she made early in their marriage and that was going into town with her hair down. Richard almost tore the hair from her head explaining, "No other man will see you like that again." It was for him and him alone. From that day forward, she wore it pinned up in a knot. She learned to live with the headaches it provided, just like she learned to live without love...

MADELINE NEVER HEARD FROM DAVID, though she knew he was somewhere in the Dakotas. Jeremiah gave her word of him every once in a while, but, that wasn't enough! On one occasion, she slipped into his cabin when he had gone into town to search for David's letters. Finding the most recent, she fingered the writing on the envelope and then brought it to her lips. Upon opening it, her eyes consumed the words —she breathed them out—

"*I have gotten work on a large ranch in Dakota Territory. Earning the respect of the owner, I quickly took to overseeing his ranch as he is down from an injury.*" Scanning further down, she read, "*I met a pretty gal named Louisa...*" She stopped. Her heart jolted. That had never occurred to her. She felt a tinge of jealousy. "*We spend a lot of time together when I'm not workin' the ranch. And even then, she follows me around like a lost puppy. She is only fifteen and fancies herself in love with me!*" Oh. Madeline laughed to herself. Poor David...or poor

Louisa! She continued,*"Lord help me...I find myself thinking of how much I miss and love...,"* A smile crossing her face...*Me*...She held the letter to her chest. "Oh, David...I miss you too..."

She heard voices and quickly put everything back as it was. Sneaking out, careful not to be seen, she heard the name "Doogan" spoken and crept closer to listen. Apparently, after all these months, McCreedy, Doogan, and Roy had been found—and killed. She felt nothing. Not gladness. Not sadness...just callousness. Richard did what he said. Hunt them down...and kill them. She shivered involuntarily. He would have done the same to David and more than likely to her had they left as she wanted so long ago.

The days blended into weeks, which blended into months. Madeline missed David so much it was hard to breathe at times. She missed his cocky grin and his unruly, golden-brown hair. She missed his tenderness but also his sly way of getting her to do what he wanted. She missed the deep rumble of his laugh—the way it resonated in his chest. It rang clear in her memory. She missed the smell of him...the smell of the outdoors and sun. Richard always smelled of scented soap.

If she closed her eyes, she could almost smell David now...hear him chuckle. She refused to let the images and sounds of him slip away... even though at times it brought her pain...pain of what she can not have. She made herself think of him throughout the days and nights. She lived in her own little world with David. Richard wasn't privy to her thoughts...there, he had no control...there, she escaped from her harsh existence.

AT ANY OPPORTUNITY, Madeline joined Mabel in the kitchen to assist in meal preparations, or she would take on a chore around the house, trying to fill her days. After all this time of living at Belle Rive, she hadn't made any friends—except Mabel and ole Jeremiah. Richard was very possessive and jealous, so she kept close to the ranch at all times. He did allow her the freedom of riding Lola over the vast acreage as long as she didn't stray too far. During those times, she would free her hair from the tight bun and ride as she did years ago back home.

Home—now there's a thought. She hadn't thought of "home" in a long time. Mostly because of memories of her father and the hurts that arose. But, there were good memories too. Memories of her mother and father taking her out riding on Sundays after changing out of their church clothes. The warm summer breeze whipped across her face as Skye galloped through the prairie grass. Those were the memories of "home" that she would try to hold onto.

Belle Rive had never become home. She always felt like a visitor walking on eggshells. She never felt like she belonged.

She and Richard rarely had any real conversation. Mostly, he would talk and she would listen. He never asked for her opinion and often ignored it if she voiced one.

One topic that did come up frequently was why she wasn't with child. He let her know how disappointed he was in her. After all, that was the reason he agreed to marry her. If she couldn't supply him with sons, then she was useless to him.

Madeline, too, was amazed at the fact that she hadn't conceived. Her mother had conceived early in her parent's marriage, so she thought she might do the same. Most of the time she was very thankful she wasn't with child, but sometimes...she longed for a baby to pour her love into and for someone who would love her back unconditionally— someone that would distract her from her pitiful life and give meaning to her days. But Richard...as a father? NO! That she could not bear to think of—fate was kind in that respect.

19

FALL

S olitude. That was all David wanted before—before Maddie, that is. Now he felt lost on a path without her. At times he thought he heard her giggle and turned to find nothing but sagebrush and prairie grass. His days in the saddle were long. He rode himself into exhaustion so sleep would find him easily. He tried praying, but his prayers felt void. Picturing Richard's hands on her about drove him insane. He hadn't felt this helpless since he was wallowing in drink and debt—out of control.

Sleep, eat, ride. That is all he did for days not knowing where he'd end up.

Late one night, he came upon a small town. The only place that showed any life was a saloon on the edge of town. He dismounted wearily and hitched Zeke to a post. Tired, with the sweat and dust of the day clinging to him, he dragged himself in. Cheap perfume, smoke, and the sweet smell of whiskey assaulted his nostrils, immediately taking him back to a time in his past. Something inside him told him to turn around and head back out of town. But he pushed it aside, strolled over to the bar, ordered a whiskey, and threw it to the back of his throat. The burning sensation of the pungent liquid caused his eyes to water. He tapped his empty glass on the counter signaling for another. He downed the second glass. Exhaling loudly, he deposited his glass down with a thud.

He turned slightly to take in the atmosphere. Because of the late hour, not many people were left. A buxom saloon girl was draped over a customer. An old codger was asleep in the corner, one foot on a chair, his mouth hanging open, a half-empty liquor bottle cradled in his lap. In the middle of the floor, his eyes landed on three men engrossed in a poker game. David's eyebrows rose. He pushed off the bar and sauntered over to the table.

"Howdy fellas," he hooked his stetson on the back of a vacant chair, "mind if I join ya?" There it was again...a quickening in his spirit. *Run!* "What's the stakes?" He slapped a wad of bills down.

Into the wee hours, they played and shared a bottle or two until David had practically wiped them out. None too happy with the newcomer, one by one they drifted out of the saloon. David stacked his bills in a nice tidy pile, stood on unsteady legs, plopped his hat on his head, and tossed some bills to the bartender to cover their drinks and more. He stumbled out the swinging doors into the cool of the morning. Not sure where he was heading, he leaned up against the post and filled his smoke-filled lungs with the crisp, fresh air. He let his eyes lazily roam the town. On the right sat the only hotel with a sign that said "No vacancy." Exhaling rather irritated, he let his head fall back, almost losing his stetson. He gazed at the sky as the stars began to vanish in the warm tones of morning. A few clouds danced across the fading moon. His gaze was drawn to the left. His bloodshot eyes fell on a cross that was illuminated by the rise of the sun. It was as if it beckoned to him. He suddenly straightened, transfixed on the sight of the orbs brilliance as it lit up the little, whitewashed church and cross. Quickly sobering, guilt and shame fell heavy on his heart; his vision began to blur. The prickly, wooden handrail bit into his palm as he clumsily lowered himself down onto the steps. *What was he doing? How could he turn back to the two vices that almost destroyed him all those years ago?*

He lifted his gaze, transfixed by the lonely cross, pointing its way to the heavens. David tried to choke down the bile that rose in his throat. He barely pulled himself up before losing all the contents of his stomach over the side of the steps. Again and again, he retched, until nothing was left inside—his grip holding fast to the splintered post, tears stinging his eyes, and his body racking with sobs. Remorse, guilt, shame, anger, sadness, bitterness, all encompassing him at once. His body hurting, muscles aching, he hauled himself upright and made his way to the little white church. The doors were unlatched. He hurried down the dimly lit aisle to the altar and dropped heavily to his knees. Hands open to God, he repented for his sin. The sin of getting drunk, the sin of gambling, the sin of hatred towards Richard...and the sin of coveting another man's wife...he was broken. While knowing he didn't deserve it, he felt God's love enveloping him. He hadn't felt such peace in a long time. He stayed as the sun rose higher and higher and the warming rays showed through the dust-covered windows. Though he hated to leave the sanctuary of the place, he rose, dropping his gambling winnings with a plunk into an offering plate. He reverently exited the building, gently closing the heavy, wooden door behind him. He felt renewed. He was forgiven.

DAVID RESUMED his trek to 'who knows where.' One fog-filled morning, he awoke to the sound of cows mooing in the distance. The sun was just beginning to burn through the haze. The chill in the air spoke of fall approaching...just how long had he been traveling? He sat up, resting his arms on bent knees. "Well, Zeke, how 'bout we see if there is a ranch close by that belongs to those moos?" Zeke grunted gently, swishing the flies away with his tail.

David rode for about a half an hour before he came upon the ranch. Trees were sparse in this flat, open prairie. He could see soft, gentle hills in the distance, but they were too far away to provide much protection from any real weather they may get out here. The cold, gray stone of the main house sat against mostly tan ground, sprinkled with soft, green mounds of grass. It made the place look cold. Hopefully, the owners are more welcoming than the home. He clicked his tongue urging Zeke forward. He could see the need for many repairs to the fence, roof, and stables...hmmm...maybe he could offer his services for a nice, warm bed and food in his belly.

An old basset hound started baying at his approach. The front door moaned and opened. David pulled on Zeke's reigns to bring him to a sudden halt. He stared as a shotgun poked out.

"What do you want?"

It wasn't the question that surprised him. It was the voice. He looked up into the face of a young lady, her face unflinching and waiting for an answer. She had a wild look about her—unkempt blond hair, half up, half falling down, and she wore britches instead of a skirt. "Howdy ma'am," David said slowly and tipped his hat.

"Keep your hands where I can see 'em." Her voice was level, face granite. "Now, answer the question."

"Well Ma'am, I just rode in and was hoping for a warm meal and a place to bed down in exchange for some work." He scanned the property, "And, if you don't mind me saying so...looks like you could use some help."

"Yeah, well we've fallin' on some hard times." She kept the shotgun level.

"The name's David Shelton, ma'am." He began to lower his hands.

"Not just yet, mister." She stepped closer. "Where ya from?"

"Nevada City. Been on the road for weeks."

"What brought ya this way?" She was unrelenting with that gun.

"Needed a change...look, ma'am. I just was hoping for a little break from the saddle. I'm plum worn out."

The girl cocked an ear towards the open door. "Just a minute, Pa!" Slowly lowering the gun, she fastened bright eyes back on David. "You seem harmless enough...dust yourself off some and water your horse. Join us inside once you're done."

With a thankful smile, David lowered his hands...finally. "Thank ya, ma'am. I'll only be a minute." He slung his heavy leg and climbed down from Zeke. Bone weary, he washed up and saw to Zeke before climbing rickety steps up to the door, which swung open as his hand rose to knock.

"Well, come on in then." The girl stepped aside and ushered him in. Pointing towards a bear of a man seated in a large, open room, she began introductions. "This here's my pa. You can call him Henry. Pa, this is David Shelton." Turning towards what David thought was the kitchen, because he smelled the most tantalizing aroma of baking bread, the girl pointed to a tall, slender woman with a baby on her hip and a spoon in her hand. "And that there's my ma, Patrice, and little brother, Daniel. Sister Molly is around here, somewheres."

"Welcome, David." Henry attempted to rise, but seeing him struggle, David rushed over to him and shook his hand.

"Pleasure to meet you, sir."

"Forgive me for not meeting ya at the door." Henry adjusted himself back down and lifted his leg and propped it up. "I've got myself an injury and can't seem to get around well anymore."

"I really appreciate the hospitality, sir." Turning towards Patrice, "Ma'am."

"And I'm Louisa," the young woman in the britches smiled...and blushed.

Uh-oh...David quirked a half-smile.

"Patrice!" Henry hollered. "When's dinner? I bet David could use some good vittles!" he chuckled.

20

DISCOVERY

The sun, streaming through the crack in the heavy curtains, made Madeline cringe. She had been dreaming a wonderful dream. David had come back for her and stole her away into the night—just like the knights of long ago would come to rescue the fair maiden. David was on a white steed, his armor glistening under the moonlight, and her long, flowing, beautiful gown blowing in the wind behind them as they flew through the night...

But now, as Madeline peeked through her eyelids, she saw that she was in the same room she shared with Richard, with all its rich, dark colors and faint cigar scent. Oh, how she hated that smell!

"Ugh. Another useless day in the life of Madeline Shelton." She moaned and threw the covers over her head, then rolled over, hoping to drift back to sleep and recapture her dream. But...no such luck. She heard Mabel rummaging around the kitchen and the smell of bacon wafting through the air. She clumsily crawled out of bed and staggered to the pitcher and basin to splash water on her sleep-heavy face. The cool liquid dripped down her neck wetting her nightgown. She shivered and silently scolded herself for not waking earlier. She knew the water would have been warm when Mabel brought it in over an hour ago. But, she had been fast asleep with a smile spread across her face.

Madeline startled when Richard flung open the door. Grabbing for her robe, she turned to him.

"Here." Richard thrust an envelope at her. "This came for you a few days ago."

"A few days ago?" Madeline snatched it, clearly irritated.

"Must have slipped my mind." He turned on his heel and left, not bothering to close the door behind him.

Feeling a little perturbed, Madeline hastily looked at the return address. It was from her father! She hurried to the door and shut it quietly and then tore into the letter.

MY DEAREST MADELINE,

I hope this letter finds you well adjusted to your new life and that you are happy.

I will never forget your face the day I sent you away. It has haunted me these two years. This is why I write to you now. To ask for your forgiveness.

Tears sprang into her eyes as she groped around for a place to sit.

I know I have no right to ask this of you, but I am a changed man, and so desire your forgiveness. I have given my life over to God and serve Him now. No more gambling. No more drinking. No more hiding out.

I have met a lady and plan to marry within the month. It's been a long time since your dear mother passed away, and I am lonely without you here. Her name is Amelia Cooper. You would like her Madeline. I hope someday the two of you can meet. It is

*with her encouragement that I write this letter that is so long
overdue.*

*I pray it is in your heart to release me from this burden I
carry.*

Love,

Your Father,

Joseph Sorrells

MADELINE SAT in disbelief as the minutes ticked by. Disbelief
that he found God. Disbelief that he was asking for her
forgiveness. Disbelief that he was getting married. *A little
late, Father, for your change, don't you think? I am the one who
had to pay for your mistake!* She was angry, not happy for
him. *And I am still paying!* She buried her face in her hands
and wept bitter tears.

Wanting nothing more than to discard the offensive
paper and never set eyes on it again, she crumpled it and
turned to burn it. Just as it was falling from her fingers, she
clasped it tightly, not ready to be done with it forever. It
screamed to her—*get your own life right with God!* And she
didn't want to do that. She was furious with her earthly
father *and* heavenly Father. She wouldn't allow either of
them room in her heart. So, she buried the offensive letter
deep under her mattress.

Madeline went through the day distracted. She tried
working in the garden, but that proved fruitless. She practically ruined everything she touched. She fought to keep the
words of her father from entering her mind, but there was
little hope for that, they consumed her. She was infuriated
with him! How dare he! She had a notion of writing him
and telling him a thing or two! And how dare he marry

someone else! What about mother? What about her memory?

Late in the day, as she was brushing down Lola, she caught a glimpse of Richard walking arm in arm with a woman she hadn't seen before—a rather tall, stately, dark-haired beauty. They seemed rather intoxicated with each other. She watched as they disappeared through the front door—Madeline's signal to stay away.

She threw down the brush and flung herself onto Lola, not bothering to saddle the horse, and flew off in a rage. This was turning out to be a terrible day. Why did Richard insist on shaming her by flaunting all these women in front of everyone as if to say she wasn't enough? Who is *this* woman? Where did she come from? Madeline was determined to find out. But, it wasn't such an easy task. Richard wasn't saying, and, so far, nobody recognized her.

ON AND ON for a couple of weeks Madeline saw the woman around, hanging on Richard's arm and seemingly on his every word. She finally discovered the woman was a Mrs. Timmons. A married woman! Richard was getting cocky and careless in his personal endeavors.

Madeline learned to keep herself occupied in her room, reading or knitting whenever Mrs. Timmons came around. Richard warned her that she is to have no contact with the woman whatsoever.

Madeline was out in the garden pulling carrots for dinner one balmy afternoon, when she saw Mrs. Timmons arrive riding side-saddle on a sleek, black mare. She had overheard some of the ranch hands talking about Mrs. Timmons earlier. Apparently, she was the wife of a Mr. Blake Timmons, a rich and powerful man fairly new to these parts. Madeline wondered what he must think of his wife running off making a fool him. She had half a mind to have a talk with Mr. Timmons, but thought better of it after considering what Richard would do if he found out. But, as it turns out, she really didn't need to concern herself with it. Shunning Sylvia turned out to be a fatal mistake for Richard. "A woman scorned..." as they say.

Apparently, Sylvia went to see Mr. Timmons, informing him of his wife's infidelity with Richard. Needless to say, Timmons had no idea and was not accustomed to being made a laughing stock. Refusing to look foolish any longer, in a rage, he seized his double barrel shotgun and headed to Belle Rive.

As night started to fall over the land, Timmons hid in the shadows, waiting for his wife and Richard to surface. Sure enough, within the hour, they waltzed out of the house laughing and carrying on. Richard took her in his arms and gave her a lingering kiss, unbeknown to them that danger lie concealed close by.

Not being able to constrain himself any longer, Timmons emerged from hiding and planted himself in front of the stunned couple. With their mouths agape and stammering for words to say, Timmons unleashed his fury with the shotgun, emptying one barrel on Richard, then the other on his wife—killing them both on the spot.

Madeline was upstairs reading when she heard the first shot. She practically dropped her book at the sudden boom. Clutching at her heart, she ran to the window just as the other shot rang out. She jumped as a scream left her throat of its own accord. She saw the lady fall in a crumble next to another body on the ground. *Richard.* She watched as ole Jeremiah and other ranch hands ran toward the scene. In the failing light, she could only assume it was Mr. Timmons

standing over both bodies, nudging with a foot, to make
sure they were dead. Two of Richard's men grabbed
Timmons and threw him on the ground. He offered no
restraint. Another man flew off on a horse towards town—
she assumed, going for the sheriff. There wasn't a need for a
doctor.

Methodically, Madeline made her way down the stairs
on trembling legs. She had never seen a dead body before,
not sure she wanted to now. But her feet kept propelling her
forward. Morbid curiosity? Or just numbness? No tears
flowed, she didn't know what she was feeling. She got to the
door, and Mabel enveloped her in a sobbing hug, her plump
body blocking the view of the slain couple. "Oh, dear, they
are both gone." Mabel sniffled. "Such a site." Madeline's
arms hung down. The whole thing was so surreal. She
brought a hand up and stiffly patted Mabel on the back and
gently pushed the woman away. Stepping around her, she
made her way over to the bodies. Vacant eyes stared up at
her. Chills ran up her spine. Jeremiah lowered himself down
and immediately shut the eyes of the pair. "Sorry, ma'am," he
mumbled, then stood in front of her, "Can I get you
anything?"

Madeline shook her head and spun around just in time
as she emptied the contents of her stomach. Mabel ran to
her and eased her back inside. Still no tears. Maybe later...
No. Probably not.

21

RETURN

D avid thought about the letter he had received from Maddie telling him of his brother's death. The only remorse he felt was that Richard probably died without the acceptance of the things of God. David shuddered at the thought, and sadness washed over his bearded face.

Choosing to focus on the letter in front of him; he now only saw the words written by Maddie's delicate hand. He had continued learning how to read and write since Maddie had started to teach him close to two years ago in that cave. The cave...all the memories of that long trek came rushing back into his mind. He could still see her tangled in the thorn bushes—screaming and carrying on. *Hadn't he told her to change into the britches he'd brought for her?* He smiled and chuckled to himself. Then the picture of when she fell into the river, and that skirt of hers snagged onto a dead tree branch almost drowning her...on and on his thoughts drifted...McCreedy and his ilk, taking her from him. The panic, the loss, and the rage that consumed him! When he had rescued her, their embrace...the kisses...the confession of

their love. Then her marriage to Richard—it carved his
heart in two. Even now, the ache he felt nearly undid him.
All ranges of emotions culminated at the memory of seeing
Maddie running from the house clutching her face...that
same rage rising up to consume him now, as it did that day
—he stole her away...only to have to return her. He couldn't
bear it. He really didn't understand why God allowed
Richard to wed her when *he* so desperately wanted to marry
her. To Richard, she was just something else he possessed.
To David, she was some*one* to be cherished and cared for.
He could not stand to think of her in Richard's arms, or
Richard striking her again...so he ran...ran from her, from
Richard, and from all that life held for him there. She chose
to stay with his brother to keep her father and him safe. But,
at what peril to her? In the end, all he could do was walk
away and give her over to God. After all, He loved her even
more than David did.

Now, after all this time, he allowed himself to dream of
what could be. Would Maddie still love him after he had
deserted her?

He longed to see her. To hold her, caress her, love her.
Would God allow it this time? He had sought answers, but
the heavens were silent.

HE HAD POURED ALL of his energy into helping Henry get his
ranch back up and running. Now that Henry had
completely healed, he was better able to care for it himself
until he could hire someone else to take David's place.
Saying his goodbyes to the family that trusted him and took
him in at a time he needed someone was harder than he
thought. David took a long, hard look around the place
feeling pride at what he had accomplished. Knowing that he

was leaving it in far better shape than when he arrived helped to relieve the sorrow of saying goodbye. But, he knew it was time to head back home. He was going back for Maddie, hoping against hope that she would still have him.

After weeks of grueling travel, David came upon the border of Belle Rive lands. He paused and drew in a deep breath, then clicked his tongue for Zeke to go forward. It still took him nearly an hour before he came into the clearing where the house sat. He scanned the distance, and seeing no one in sight, made his way to the family cemetery. He dismounted Zeke and walked over to the most recently dug grave. It was starting to grow weeds and grass on it. He wasn't surprised that no one tended it. Richard wasn't well-liked by anyone. He was only feared. David shook his head sadly. The sky threatened rain, and there was a chill in the air—very fitting for standing at the grave-site of Richard his cold, callous brother. He was in such deep thought that he didn't hear her come up behind him.

Then she spoke. "David?"

He turned suddenly at Maddie's voice. She wore a simple, black dress with her hair pulled up in a severe knot on the back of her head, much like the first day he met her. She had aged in the last two years, looking older than her twenty-one years. He cringed inside knowing who was responsible. Richard got his comeuppance in the end. Too bad it wasn't by David's hand, but, God would not allow it. He hated Richard for what he did to Maddie and others. Even at his grave, David felt no loss of his brother. *He had to work on his forgiveness.*

How small and distant the woman before him looked. There were no tears, but there was a sadness there. Looking straight into her eyes, he could tell she was glad to see him.

He smiled and began to close the gap between them. He reached for her hands.

She stiffened. "Madeline...Maddie, forgive me for stayin' away so long." He bent down to kiss her cheek.

Her face flushed under his touch. When her eyes met his, a tiny spark sprung to life in her soul, even though it was just for a moment. He had come back. But, was it too late? She had withered away inside and out. The fire that once intrigued David had been extinguished. Will he see anything left in her to salvage?

Her face was carefully void of emotion. "David, I'm so glad you've come. It is good to see you. It has been too long." She looked up into his gentle eyes.

"I came as soon as I could."

"Please, come to the house. I need to sit for a while." She reached up to rub her temple as she turned to lead him toward the house.

It's that hairdo again, he thought. Then, reaching up, he grabbed the two pins that caused her such discomfort and released her flowing, brown hair to fall in soft curls down her back.

She whirled around instantly with her hands flying to the back of her head. A look of shock on her face, she said, "Richard wouldn't like that."

"Richard's dead, Maddie," he reminded her, then tossed the pins aside.

She looked like she might object, then stopped herself. There *was* immediate relief as the pain in her temple slipped away. She didn't see the smile that played across his face.

And he didn't see hers.

22

RENEWAL

Madeline led David to the great room and offered him a seat across from her. They sat in awkward silence for a time; only the ticking of the clock could be heard.

"The funeral was...nice," Madeline offered, "though not too many people came." She dropped her eyes to look at her folded hands in her lap.

"I really don't care about the funeral," David said bluntly. Her head shot up, eyes locking onto his for meaning. Studying her face, he continued. "I wanna know about you. How are *you*?"

She lowered her gaze again, feeling uncomfortable with his steady gaze on her. "I am...doing all right." She looked back up. "There is a lot to do around here to keep me busy."

"The truth, please." Silence.

David swallowed hard and cleared his throat. He stood up and walked over to her. Then, sitting next to her, said, "Maddie, ya have to know—I came back for you...for you, alone. You are no longer bound to my brother—yer a free woman. Yer father's debts are no more."

Her heart started pounding at his words. Dare she hope? How can this be? After she turned her back on God when she felt He deserted her, could He really be giving her back her heart's desire? No. It can't be. Forcing her heartbeat to slow, she turned slightly toward him. "I am a broken woman, David. I have nothing left to offer you. Your brother took all that I was and am."

"I don't believe that." He shook his head and clasped her small hands in his large, calloused ones.

"Look at me, David," she said, removing her hands from his and dropping them to her lap. "The girl you knew is no more." Tears started to spring into her eyes. "She was lost just after she wed your brother...and you...and God left her." Her dark hair cascaded forward as she hung her head.

Those words cut David to the bone. He understood how she felt about him, but not about God. "Maddie, God has never left you...you left Him. All those times you thought He was ignorin' ya, He was wantin' you to draw closer to Him— to let Him be yer everything and fill those empty places in yer heart. But instead, ya filled 'em up with anger, bitter- ness...and grief. You shut *Him* out; yet got mad when He didn't answer ya the way you wanted Him to. He's always been there—when yer mom died, and yer brother. When yer dad gambled and drank and when he sent ya off to pay a debt he should have paid—even when Richard made you his wife. God wanted to comfort you durin' all those times."

Madeline sat quietly, taking in all that David was saying. At first, she had tensed up, not wanting to hear about God— didn't want to hear the truth. Truth...now there's a thought. She could feel her heart softening. Tears began to gather and slowly spilled forth, falling to her folded hands.

"Oh, Maddie, open yer heart to Him again," David pleaded. "Let Him have all that pain and sorrow."

The flood gates opened, and she buried her face in her hands. David gathered her in his arms. He held her for a long time, stroking her hair, and praying silently.

She felt safe in David's arms; how she had longed and dreamed of being wrapped in their strength again. But now, it was as if God *Himself* was holding her and ministering to all those hurts and lost dreams. As she let down the barriers holding her captive, she felt Him filling all the recesses of her broken heart with His peace. His love, coming in waves, caressing her being. She had never really known Him until now. She had been nothing more than a spoiled brat demanding the God of the universe to bend to her every whim. The realization made her cry all the more. Not out of condemnation, but brokenness. She had lost so much time with Him.

Madeline stayed in David's embrace for what seemed like hours. The sun began to break through the dismal sky. The heavens were speaking. David knew in his heart of hearts she was to be his. He slipped off the settee to kneel in front of her.

She smiled, embarrassed. "Look at me...I must be a mess."

"I *am* lookin' at you," love clearly showing on his handsome, bearded face, "and I've never seen anythin' more beautiful." He leaned forward and gently cupping her face, kissed her. She did not pull away...instead wrapped her arms around his neck. Her sweet kiss intertwined with salt from her tears. David leaned back slightly, his thumbs brushed away the tears, and then he gently kissed her forehead. Then, he tilted her head up so he could look her in the eyes. He breathed, "I love you, Maddie—I have for a long time now. I want ya to be my wife. Please, marry me?"

Her heart soared with joy so full it was hard to contain.

A brilliant smile lit up her face as she cried, "Yes, David, I will marry you."

"Tonight," David said.

"Tonight?" uncertainty in her voice. "Why, David Shelton! I can't marry you tonight...we just buried Richard some weeks ago, and there's too much planning..."

"Maddie, don't make me wait. It already feels like a lifetime."

This is what she always wanted. David, as her husband. Why wait? She had such a peace in her heart, finally. God had made her whole within hours and now was offering her heart's desire.

"All right, David. Tonight." She was suddenly on her feet, practically knocking David over. "Let me tell Mabel we have a wedding to plan!" She was as giddy as a schoolgirl, about to take flight, when David stood and reached for her hand, drawing her to him. "I'll send for the Parson." He kissed her like a wife should be kissed which stole her breath...

She put her arms up between them and gently pushed away. "I...I can't think when you do that."

He grinned. He was having trouble clearing his head too.

"My, won't the Parson be surprised. A funeral of one husband, and now a wedding to his brother all within a month." She looked a little concerned.

"Awww Maddie, don't ya worry yer pretty little head about it. I'll take care of everythin' darlin'."

She blushed at the way he called her darlin'. Then, with a permanent smile etched on her features, darted away to find Mabel.

23

WEDDING

The simple, black dress lay crumpled in a corner. Madeline now adorned the soft, yellow dress she wore so long ago—the one she had packed away and refused ever to wear again. It held memories of hope and budding love that were dashed so cruelly by her marriage to Richard. Now, she smiled again. Her trembling hands smoothed the wrinkles long gone. Her eyes rose slowly latching onto her reflection in the mirror before her. A pale, thin-looking stranger stared back at her. The last two years had not been kind. Then, she focused on her eyes and caught a gleam...a spark of life long absent. She pinched her cheeks to bring some color to the bland palette. Her soft, brown locks shone brilliantly in the dimly lit room. She had only a few strands pinned gently away from her face. The rest hung in soft curls down her slender back. Taking in a deep, calming breath, she turned with a swish of her skirt and left her room, descending the steps to her future.

· · ·

If the Parson found it somewhat strange to be coming back to Belle Rive so soon after Richard's funeral, he didn't say. He was the one that had officiated over Richard's wedding to Madeline and knew of the situation that had brought it about. He had to have seen the look of horror written on Madeline's face as he pronounced them man and wife. David stood talking with the man as he awaited his bride. He seemed genuinely happy for them.

David heard an upstairs door latch and saw Mabel give him a knowing smile. It was time. He didn't know what to do with his hands. As soon as Maddie came into view, his throat went dry. She was a vision. He was scared to blink or draw breath, thinking that the apparition would vanish. But, her shimmering, brown eyes fastened onto his, and she smiled shyly. He watched as she drew closer, barely constraining himself not to rush to her. *Patience.* Then, ever so graceful, she stood in front of him. He reached for her small hands and enveloped them in his, then gently brushed her forehead with his lips.

They had a small, quiet ceremony with only Mabel and Jeremiah serving as witnesses. Mabel kept dabbing at her eyes and blowing her nose.

"I now pronounce you husband and wife." Turning to David, the Parson said, "You may kiss your bride."

David, still clasping Maddie's hands, gathered her to himself. Ever so gently, his mouth touched hers. She tasted of candied apples. He longed to linger there, but knew he'd have a lifetime of kissing her. Reluctantly, he broke free. He grinned down at her blushing upturned face and whispered, "I love you, Mrs. Shelton."

"Mrs. *David* Shelton," she smiled in return. "And, I love you." Though her married name was the same, the man before her certainly was not. Here, stood a man of honor, strength, and kindness, capable of so much love. Richard was greedy, powerful, ruthless, and didn't know what the word love meant.

They turned around, Madeline hugging a sniffling Mabel and David shaking hands with a beaming Jeremiah. The Parson heartily congratulated them. Then they all made their way to the dining area for supper and cake which Mabel had put together as soon as she heard there was to be a wedding.

Laughter and joy rang through the halls, a promise of much happier days ahead. Madeline had never looked more radiant or content as they bid their guests goodbye and goodnight. Jeremiah was to take the Parson into town and take Mabel to her daughter's home for the night. She would be back bright and early to see that the newlyweds would have some decent breakfast.

Once they had the house to themselves, David lifted Madeline into his arms and carried her up the stairs to her special room. What had been her refuge in a world of chaos, would now become their bedroom.

Mabel had drawn the curtains before she left and lit two oil lanterns. She had sprinkled fragrant rose petals from the garden all over their bed. The sight was enchanting. David sat Madeline carefully on the edge of their bed—kissed her, then left her to ready herself.

She felt a little giddy and nervous as she dressed into the pale green gown she bought when she and David stopped in that town so long ago, but had never worn. At the time she bought it, she had planned to wear it on her wedding night for Richard, even though she secretly pretended it was for David. That was when she first began to realize she had feelings for him.

Smiling at the memory, she brushed her hair until it glistened. She wanted tonight to be perfect.

When David re-entered, Madeline was turning down the lanterns. She was a sight to behold. He walked to her and taking her hands gently in his, he led her to their bed. "My wife," he whispered huskily as he kissed her trembling lips.

MADELINE WAS the first to wake. As her sleepy eyes fluttered open, she stared at the man in front of her. *Was this a dream?* She had seen this face many times in her sleep before, only to wake up and find it a cruel trick in the night. She reached over to touch the face. It was warm under her fingertips. The memories of yesterday flooded back into her mind...David came back...it really was him. He was here...lying beside her. *Her husband*...and like the knight of her dreams, he had stolen her away into the night.

She replayed the wedding in her mind. It was short but beautiful. She thought of how handsome he had looked standing beside her. His beard, which he had grown since she saw him last, was short and trimmed. His curls, pushed back away from his face, refusing to be tamed, still strove to touch his shoulders. He wore a new pair of tan pants with a dark blue shirt. He was not flashy, like Richard. He was...he was David. The man she loved more than life itself.

She blushed at the thought of last night. David was gentle and kind, showing her how much he loved and desired her. They found each other throughout the night, hardly believing they were actually in each other's arms.

David...her husband, she smiled, was a wondrous man. She had never been able to express herself as she did last night. He made it easy, drawing out the real Madeline. She had never known such love and acceptance. She snuggled closer to him and drifted back to sleep...a feeling of contentment...wholeness...completeness.

EPILOGUE

Three months later, Madeline was standing at the train station weeping and hugging her father. With all the love that David had shown her—and God had poured into her—how could she not forgive her father? She wrote to him a week after her wedding. The letter contained many watermarks from her tears, but, with much hope for the future, she gushed words of forgiveness, and a desire to see him and meet his bride.

David watched Joseph Sorrell's water-filled eyes overflow as he clutched his daughter to himself and wept. God truly did a miracle. Close to three years ago, David despised this man and never thought to see any emotion for his daughter whatsoever erupt from him. Now, there was no hiding it. He was a changed man, and he loved his daughter —and the daughter loved and forgave her father.

David, a man not prone to tears, found himself wiping a stray tear off his cheek. Amelia Sorrells had no pretense. She was crying right along with them—such joy filled her eyes.

.   .   .

As BEAUTIFUL AS the reunion earlier that day between father and daughter was, nothing was as beautiful to David as his wife was at this moment. After a long and emotional day, they got her father and Amelia settled into a guest room and retired early. Madeline led him to sit on the bed, and she knelt down in front of him. "I love you *so* much, David." She reached for his hands and pulled them to her face. "God had been very good to me." Her soft, brown eyes closed for a moment. Drawing a steady breath, she continued, "He blessed me with a wonderful, caring husband... and now...He has blessed our union." Her eyes fluttered up to meet his. Her husband stared blankly at her, not entirely understanding what she had just said. She sighed, "David, you're going to be a father."

A huge grin spread across his bearded features as the realization of what she just said hit him. He leaped to his feet, sweeping her up into his arms and spinning around the room. *Thank goodness her stomach wasn't queasy!* Madeline squealed in delight.

Thoughts of God's love rushed over her. He had brought her full circle—first with Him, then by bringing David back into her life, and finally restoring her relationship with her earthly father. God was good. So very, very good.

"And I will restore to you the years that the locusts hath eaten..."
Joel 2:25

THE END

COWBOY LINGO

Understanding Cowboy Lingo
    prairie tenors – Coyotes
    auger – boss
    big bug - boss
    consumption – tuberculosis
    dirk – knife
    flea trap – bedroll
    gut warmer – whiskey
    spell – long time
    balderdash – nonsense, foolishness
    buzzard food – dead
    bed him down – dead
    beef – dead
    bushwacked – a cowardly attack or ambush
    airin' the lungs – cursing
    hold your horses – stay calm
    buffaloed – confused
    don't get your dander up – anxious, excited
    get your back up – to get angry
    get a wiggle on – hurry

high tail – ride at full speed
high, falutin – fancy, pompous
bellyache – complain
hanker – strong wish or want
have a mind to – to be willing, to have a notion
barkin' at a knot – wasting time, useless
reckon – guess, think
feller – fellow
nohow – not at all, noway
yammerin' – talking
atwixt – between

ACKNOWLEDGMENTS

Thank you to my Heavenly Father. Thank you for giving me this story and the ability to write it. Thank you to my husband, Paul, for all your love and support. (And help editing!) You're my favorite! Thank you to my mom, Barbara, for all your prayers and encouragement. You're my biggest fan! Thank you to Misti Konsavage for your awesome editing skills. And thank you to Hosanna Emily for your help along the publishing road. Thank you to Jordan Jung for creating the beautiful cover and capturing just what I wanted. And thank you to my many friends and family members that took the time to read this story and give me valuable feedback.

You can email me at : kimamarch94@gmail.com

Check out Jordan's work at: www.jordandenae.com

ABOUT THE AUTHOR

Kim A. March is a wife, a mother of 3 grown children—plus 2 sons in law, and a mamaw of a precious, beautiful grand daughter. She loves reading & listening to audiobooks. (Swoons at a good love story!) Jesus, pizza, coffee, travel, and watching UFC! (Mixed Martial Arts). Hates exercise. She is a proud Military BRAT. She makes her home in South Central Kentucky.

Made in the USA
Monee, IL
30 March 2020

24151263R00088